Reflections

The Christmas Collection

Paul John Hausleben

Cover design, the cover concept, and computer software retouch and enhancement of images by Paul John Hausleben
Photographs by Paul John Hausleben

Published by God Bless the Keg Publishing
Somewhere, U.S.A.

ISBN: 978-0-9906979-3-0

Dedication

To those dark, dull days, before Christmas

Reflections
The Christmas Collection

The Old Soldier's Christmas Faith
Featuring Pastor Paul John Henson and other characters from the Adventures of Harry and Paul

Where the Cold Wind Whistles
A Christmas tale

The Radio
Featuring the old man and other characters from the Adventures of Harry and Paul

In the Fields
A Christmas tale for children of all ages. Featuring Pastor Paul John Henson and other characters from the Adventures of Harry and Paul

The Number Fourteen
A Christmas Tale

The Return of the Time Bomb in The Cupboard
Featuring Ronzo Boatmann, the old man, and other characters from the Adventures of Harry and Paul

Contents

Acknowledgements

A warm thank you to the Christmas season of 2014. It gave me time to reflect and to think. For that, I will always be very grateful.

"The reflections of that wonderful time so long ago, were mirrors to my past, but they were also lenses to my future."

Paul John Hausleben

December 2014

Preface

Without a doubt, the last book that I wanted to write in my career was another blasted, bloomin,' Christmas collection! That was until a few short days ago, when much to my surprise, and my own apprehension, I wrote this short anthology.

This sad tale of woe began a week or so before Christmas of 2014. It started with an outstanding picture that I snapped with a new camera that I purchased during the Christmas season. I zoomed in close and snapped a photograph of a red Christmas ornament hanging on my little Christmas tree. I studied the picture, and the glow of the many-colored lights in the glass of the ornament was striking. Lo-and-behold, under careful study, there was a reflection of me in the glass too. You could clearly see in the picture, the camera as well as my hand on the camera and part of my dopey face, while I was happily snapping the picture. A big smile arrived on that same dopey face because I thought that it was an awesome photograph.

Then a dose of Christmas induced doom struck me.

I leaned back and my thoughts drifted . . . reflections of Christmas. I thought to myself, what a great title for a Christmas book and what a wonderful picture to use on the cover.

Oh no! Why did I think of that?

Why did I snap this bloody picture?

Why, Hausleben, why do you do these things? Thorny holly and a maze of ivy just entrapped you in a Christmas snare, along with endless renditions of that much beloved song, "Silver Bells" to echo above your head as a backdrop of misery while you compose your latest drivel.

When I initially set out to release some inspiration on these pages, I tried hard to convince myself that this would merely be a winter collection of stories.

Yes, winter that is it! A winter theme will avoid another Christmas collection.

Good luck with that Hausleben because Christmas made an appearance in the very first title of the first story that I wrote! Therefore, it started, and in a marathon writing session, during the Christmas season of 2014, I wrote this entire collection in two days.

It was both exhausting and exhilarating all at the same time.

Oh, the madness, Christmas, Christmas, Christmas. The holiday haunts me. I do not even celebrate it very much these days. I long ago gave Christmas up as being just another day, just another tainted mess that the media, organized religion, the retailers, and in fact, mankind, has managed to create.

Yet, it still haunts me, because the memories linger so strongly. Yes, I think that despite my best efforts, Christmas will always follow me around endlessly. It really does because it sends such powerful ghosts to disturb me.

My family, especially my father (the inspiration for the character of "the old man") celebrates the Christmas season with great exuberance and they provided me with a lifetime of wonderful memories because of their efforts. It has brought me such joy and such raw emotion over my life; I imagine that my best defense is to admit defeat and understand that the Christmas season will never let me go.

I tried very hard to resist composing this drivel, but there is something about Christmas, of which just inspires me to write of my memories, of my joy, and to a certain extent, of my hope. I think what I am really trying to do is release my own emotion from my soul and share my experiences with you, the reader.

I wish that I could promise that this will be the last Christmas book, Christmas collection or other holiday related claptrap, of which I will put between covers. Yet the lure is great, and somehow, I might find myself lured once again into a trap of holly and ivy. Not to mention that wonderful, melodious song. . ..

Therefore, I make no promises, nor do I make any advance apologies, my dear reader.

It is my hope that you enjoy reading this collection as much as I enjoyed writing it.

Thank you for reading it.

Paul John Hausleben

December 2014

Prologue

When the Christmas season appears on the horizon, many people rejoice with the exuberance of the arrival of their favorite time of the year, while others moan and groan and their wallets and credit lines quiver and tremble with the mere mention of the arrival of the blessed day. Amongst the disappointed and non-joyful calendar watchers, there lies the apprehension and foreboding of the arrival of January bills. Yet despite their lack of exuberance for the holiday, the moaners and groaners open their wallets for the retail world to raid and pillage. They open these same wallets, to reach in and grab handfuls of some hard-earned cash or unhappily extend more credit, which they should not extend, all in the yearly quest to purchase Christmas gifts. Gifts, which a week or so after the joyful day has passed, are quickly forgotten and then finally, and somewhat unceremoniously, tossed into corners of dark closets by the end of January of the following year. Still, you can always say that you gave Uncle Winfred and Aunt Huffnpuff *something* for Christmas last year.

Nowadays, Christmas makes its first appearance in September or even in late August. The media and the retailers cannot help themselves. The madness known as the modern media and the retail world is no longer content to settle for just Christmas or the holidays for words to describe the season, they have now created fantastic catch phrases and buzzwords for the various "important" days of the season.

Let us see, we have, "Super Saturday," "Black Friday," "Cyber Monday," "Gift Card Day," and a host of other alluring names for these "extra special" days.

When the eggnog boils down to a thick paste, and a nip or two of Christmas cheer sipped from a shot glass kicks into your bloodstream, the key is to overlook the best efforts of the modern world to spoil the glorious spirit of the season known as Christmas.

Despite Christmas being a holiday of very suspicious origins, with the obvious pagan roots, now passed off and morphed into a Christian celebration, Christmas still has merit. If one were to overlook the dubious entanglement of organized religion in proposing this to be "the birthday of Jesus," the basic premise of the coming of the Savior, combined with faith, joy, peace on Earth, goodwill, well, you know the rest of the scoop, are certainly worthwhile causes and filled with emotions and hope.

We need not to be afraid to stick our hands deep in the prickly holly and resist the entanglement of a maze of ivy. It is actually not a bad idea at all, to dig just a little deeper under the surface of the materialistic marketing of a beleaguered Christmas.

When we do that, look at what we will find!

Christmas, glorious Christmas!

Do you know something? Perhaps it was actually there all the time.

The Old Soldier's Christmas Faith

"Thank you dear, Martha. Please, now go home and enjoy the rest of the day with your family. I will see you later for the Christmas Eve service."

My faithful assistant, Mrs. Martha Wiggins, frowned a bit at me as she handed me a piece of paper printed with the address of the last shut-in parishioner of Reunion Lutheran Church for me to visit for Christmas this year. Martha was my right-hand person in the daily operation of Reunion Lutheran Church, who along with my facility manager, Mr. Dave Sharp, combined their best efforts and tried their very best to keep me on track and from falling into a deep abyss of my usual eccentric behavior and outlandishly strange situations.

"Now, you know how I love you dearly, Pastor Paul, but are you sure you have this all straight now? You have a tendency to stray into disorganization without my help. Do you know how to get to his house? The afternoon is waning so quickly now and if you become lost on the way to his house, then the day will be gone, and you have to return here for services. Mr. Tilley does not require a visit today. He will understand how busy you are during the season. You can visit him after Christmas. You should be home early too and spend a little time with Binky and the children on Christmas Eve. Dear Pastor Paul, I must say that you work too hard!"

I smiled at Martha and her concern. I gently took the paper from her, led her by the hand to the closet outside of our offices, and opened it. Taking her winter coat and hat, I made a hand motion for her to spin around while I placed her coat upon her and gently placed her hat in her hands.

"Martha, please, I assure you that I will be fine. I will find Mr. Tilley's house with no trouble, pay him a quick visit, and be back here in a flash. Thank you for your concern and your superior organizational skills. Please go home early today."

Martha smiled and said, "Well, if you insist. Now, please be on your way quickly, Pastor Paul. Do you have everything you need?"

"Sure do, Martha. I am on top of my game today. I laid it all out ahead of time. I am putting my winter coat and hat on because I know Binky will watch me leave in the jeep and she will scold me if she catches me wearing only a vest. I am shutting off the lights and heading out now."

We both walked towards the exit of the church offices and I closed all the doors behind me while we walked.

Martha turned, looked at me, and checked my hands.

"Ah, your communion kit, Pastor Paul."

I stopped in my tracks, gave a little wiggle of my mouth and a snap of my fingers.

"Left it in my office . . . thank you, Martha."

She laughed and waved her hands at me.

"Top of your game, eh, Pastor Paul? I will see you later. Drive safely."

I laughed and yelled back to her as I ran towards my office, "Martha, you have been sent to me from Heaven. Straight from Heaven, my dear Martha!" A quick jaunt brought me back to my office, where I grabbed the communion kit and hustled my way back out to where I had parked my jeep in the parking lot of Reunion Lutheran Church.

It was a dull, dark day before Christmas right around 1993 and Martha was, of course, correct. I needed to finish this mission and return home to the parsonage to spend a little time with my wife and two children on Christmas

Eve. I had a long list of shut-in church members to visit this year and I had worked my way through all of them except for Mr. Tilley. He was the only remaining member on my list.

I climbed up inside the cab of my old, trusty jeep and closed the rag top door. This old vehicle and I had been to what seemed like the top of the world and back, but I would not trade it in for the finest vehicle in the world. There is no way any vehicle could have the character of this old set of rusty bolts and wheels.

We had shared too much together, both good and bad, over the years.

I started the engine; put the stick shift into gear and slowly pulled out of the parking lot of the church. I looked over towards the parsonage to see if I could see my wife, Binky, through the kitchen window, where she often watched my comings and goings from the church, but I did not see her at her "post" this afternoon. Perhaps Martha had already assured her that she would place me back on track when I derailed and Binky relaxed, knowing that Martha was on her game.

I had spoken with Binky right before lunch, and she knew of my plans to visit Mr. Tilley and then return home before Christmas Eve services. My wife had told me that she was planning to work on some Christmas crafts with our two children, Heather Sarah and Paul William, and then bake cookies and prepare other culinary delights, for not only our Christmas Eve and day feast but also for Boxing Day.

My dear Mum's holiday and my English heritage had come in handy now that I had become a Lutheran pastor. Since I was now busy working every Christmas Eve and Christmas Day, we tabled our larger holiday celebrations until the day after Christmas, or what some areas of the world call Boxing Day.

Binky is a fabulous cook, and she whipped up delights

for not only your mind, stomach and taste buds to enjoy, but she created lifetime memories with her holiday feasts.

Our best friends, Rose and Harry M. Redmond Junior and their little girl, Blue Cloud, my parents, my in-laws, our close friends, Ronzo and Linny Boatmann and many others, looked forward to visiting our house on Boxing Day for the festivities.

This year would be no exception!

We shared food, laughter, memories, and a few Big Boulder beers. Of course, Ronzo would have a few Dingleberry beers, but the rest of us would skip them, since the rest of us considered them too sweet for our taste.

I turned the jeep out onto the main highway and made my way north onto the roadway. Mr. Tilley lived more towards the center of the town where Reunion was located in Hibernian, New Jersey. The church was in a rural area on the outskirts of the town, hidden deep in an enclave of beauty and natural wonder. The setting was a large part of why Binky and I loved the church so much. The setting was as if God had carved a hole in the New Jersey forests and inspired the congregation to locate the church property in that special spot. It truly brought glory to the Lord.

Even though it was only a little past one in the afternoon; it was already dark. I had my headlights on and street lights flickered on along the roadways. I could see the glow of homes decorated in festive Christmas light displays and the occasional, obligatory, grinning plastic Santa Claus accompanied by his happy plastic reindeer, perched upon a lawn here and there.

It was very cold now; the little heater on my jeep struggled to put out even a few spurts of heat. Good thing that I enjoyed it cold because this was the perfect vehicle for me. Heat was truly an option.

It had snowed a little a few days earlier, but now the only remains of the snow were dirty piles of corn snow lying jagged and frozen and gathered along the edges of the roads here and there, and some patches deep in the shady areas of the landscape. As I rolled towards Mr. Tilley's house, I thought hard about what I knew about this particular church member.

I was ashamed to say that it was not too much.

I knew that he was a military man; he had a disability, in which I believed to be war related, and then due to some type of prolonged illness, he became more of a shut-in as the years had progressed. He had attended services a few years ago, when I first arrived at Reunion, but now he no longer attended services on a regular basis. This was my first visit to his home. He had an elder assigned to his care, and Mr. Tilley had expressed an interest to the elder to have a pastoral visit for Christmas.

I felt a bit guilty for not staying on top of the situation better, but without an assistant pastor, the pastoral duties of Reunion Lutheran Church had grown to be a bit overwhelming. Since Binky and I had first arrived at Reunion, the church had progressed from being a target for closing to a membership that was now bursting at the seams. Due to the explosion of the membership, we recently had added a newly constructed addition on the sanctuary, as well as our fellowship and education halls, and the horizon was indeed quite rosy!

My boss, the famous Bishop Werner Beck Clodhopper Von Houten, had strongly suggested that it was now time to call an assistant pastor to help me with the duties, but we had not moved much past some initial discussions on the subject.

I down-shifted the jeep while I picked up the paper that Martha had given me with the directions printed upon it. I drove and occasionally glanced at the directions while working hard to keep my eyes on the roadway.

Good. I had taken the correct exit. I pulled off on the side of the road that I had turned onto and stopped. I put my safety flashers on while I glanced at the rest of the directions. A mile or two, make a right turn on Cedar Street, then a quick left to Fox Run Court and Mr. Tilley's house, was number ten Fox Run Court.

Even I could handle this one.

I made the last few turns into a small subdivision and quickly found number ten Fox Run Court. I pulled my jeep into the small driveway, slid the stick shift into gear, and shut off the engine. Glancing at my watch, I saw that I actually arrived a few minutes early. Martha had made the appointment for around one thirty in the afternoon, and it was twenty minutes past the hour.

Assuring myself that Mr. Tilley would not mind that I was early, I grabbed my Bible and the communion kit and made my way to the front porch of the home. I had shed my winter coat and decided to leave it in the jeep, so my black suit and collar were fully exposed. I had a fleeting thought for a moment or two that perhaps Mr. Tilley would relay information to my wife, and squeal on me that I did not wear my winter coat, but the thoughts quickly left my mind.

The house was small, but unique, in that you did not see many of these types of designs in houses nowadays. It was a dark wood, "arts and crafts" type home, maybe around fifteen hundred square feet or thereabouts in size. The home had a large, open porch and delightfully colored stained-glass windows in various locations, around the entire home such as above the doors and above the porch.

It was a striking home.

When I reached the front door, and went to ring the doorbell, the door suddenly swung open and a short, thin-faced, elderly man stood there staring at me. He supported himself on a wooden cane. He had pulled the front door open with such force that a small Christmas wreath nailed on the front door flapped and bounced on the surface of the door. I recognized the chap standing in front of me as Mr. Tilley.

"C'mon in, Pastor Paul. You are early! I like when a man is early. Especially a pastor. Youse guys usually are late because you are dreaming of Heaven and saving souls and other such ridiculous thoughts! The Lord saves souls and provides admittance to Heaven, not long-haired pastors from old Paterson City. You are simply the sideline coaches."

I had forgotten how Mr. Tilley had some very strong opinions and that he spoke his mind rather strongly and quite often.

"C'mon, c'mon, shake your long-haired ass and get on in here. My furnace is going to turn on if you let all my heat out. Oil costs a small fortune these days. Damn rip-off because of those greedy-ass oil company bastards."

I stepped up the pace, smiled at the old chap's observations and walked into the home while quickly closing the door behind me.

"Good afternoon, Mr. Tilley. You are looking well." I extended my hand and the elderly man braced himself on his cane and shook my hand with fervor.

"No coat, Pastor Paul? Not good, I hear your wife makes notes of such things!"

Oh, oh! My first miscalculation was the extent of my wife's influence. I smiled at him but did not answer. I imagined that I was doomed, anyway.

"I must say that your wife is quite a looker. Forgive me, but she is a fantastic-looking woman. My wife was gorgeous, too. There is a picture of her on the wall there."

He braced himself against the wall, took the end of his cane and pointed towards a picture in the living room of a smiling woman with long, curly hair. I turned and admired the photograph. Mr. Tilley was correct because the woman in the picture was gorgeous.

"Thank you for the compliment, and I have to say that I agree with you on both of your observations."

"Please come to the living room, where we can sit, relax,

and we can talk for a bit."

He then moved for the first time, and I somewhat awkwardly went ahead of him, not really knowing if I should stop and help him or if he would be insulted at my offer. Mr. Tilley may be disabled, but he surely was no winky dink!

This was a tough old bird.

I could tell.

So far, in my life, I have met quite a few of them.

He barely moved, and he shuffled his feet and legs slowly while bracing his weight on the cane and moving in a rather uncomfortable and out-of-control manner. I decided the best course of action was to ignore his disability and make my way to a chair.

First, I set the small communion kit on a table and then selected a chair, stood next to it and waited for him to arrive before I sat down. I held my Bible in my hands and relaxed while I watched him make slow and steady progress. Mr. Tilley made his way into the room and sat in a chair opposite me.

"Well, go ahead and sit ya tall, n'skinny ass on down, there, Pastor Paul."

Mr. Tilley held his cane up, pointed at the chair behind me, and waved it in the air while he smiled. His eyes were bright blue and his thin face somehow reflected the color of them. The very top of his head had just some thin wisps of white hair upon it, and the hairs were a bit tossed and sticking up from his head. While he sat in the chair, he reached up to smooth the hairs and make sure they were all flat on the top of his head.

The living room had Christmas decorations all around and they broadcasted a rather festive feeling of Christmas in the somewhat dark home. There was a small, but gaily lit, and meticulously decorated Christmas tree, set upon a table in the corner of the room. There were strings of pine garland, a few wreaths, and some twinkling lights hung from a fireplace mantle. Flickering, electric candles illuminated all the windows, and the lights of the candles cast a festive glow upon the perimeter of the room. A radio sitting at a table played some Christmas music softly in the background. The fireplace had a small fire glowing inside of it; I observed that the wood inside of the fireplace had almost reached the end of the line; however, it still projected warmth that filled the room.

Mr. Tilley caught my eyes wandering the room, and he read my thoughts.

"Nice decorations, right? Not bad for an old guy who can barely move. I do it all myself, and I have for all of these years. I will decorate for Christmas as long as I can breathe, Pastor Paul. It keeps me lost in my memories. That is what Christmas is all about for me now. It is about music, faith, and memories of the past."

"It is wonderful, Mr. Tilley. In fact, I have to say that it is quite a spectacular holiday setting," I said while still admiring the inside of the home and festive decor.

"Thank you. I keep myself moving. That is the key to all of life once you reach my age, Pastor Paul. I keep moving. Slow but steady and even clean the joint on my own. As far as the yard work goes though, I pay a young boy from around the corner who cuts the grass for me and shovels my front walks when it snows. I just need help with my food shopping because I cannot make it to the store. You see, I have not driven a car for years now, therefore, I pay a gal from church and she is kind enough to go for me. She insists that she should do it for no dough, but I will not hear of it. I throw her a few bucks to cover her costs. She is some cute little chickee poo from the home mission group you started when you first got to Reunion. She wears tight shirts that hug her breasts and keep my eyes sharp, and my heart beating!"

I chuckled at his profound humor and honesty. Mr. Tilley leaned back in his chair and smiled as too, chuckled at his own comments.

"Forgive my painful honesty and my offensive language, Pastor Paul. However, you are, after all, just a man, such as I am too. I ain't no phony and speak the same to a pastor as I do to any other man."

Mr. Tilley looked at me to gauge my reaction. I nodded to acknowledge that I agreed that his statements were correct.

Satisfied at my response, he continued, "It has saved my life. I swear it has. Not the cute chickee poo, but the overall mission of the church. You run a tight ship there, Pastor Paul. I think God sent you to Reunion to save not only the church, but to save old boys such as I am. I had my doubts when I first met you . . . hairy guy, beard, some type of hippie weirdo. Then I heard you preach and saw the look in your eyes. I knew. You are a man of God, pastor, no doubt in my mind at all. I know men. I have seen evil, seen good, and seen the face of God here on Earth. I know it. I swear."

"Thank you, Mr. Tilley, I appreciate the kind remarks. I have to say that I have contributed the least to the success of Reunion, it has been a collective effort."

"Oh, bullshit, Pastor Paul! I may not be able to attend services all the time, but I listen to the tapes of the services and I still have connections. The word is that you are the man."

I did not comment, but I smiled. Mr. Tilley was a kick. I rather liked the old chap; he was honest and full of that "tough guy" New Jersey spirit. I opened my Bible and felt his eyes studying me while I thumbed through it, until I reached the Christmas story in the Book of Luke. I wanted to change the subject from Pastor Paul John Henson to the word of God.

"Well now, let's read a bit about what these next few days are really all about for us. In those days, Caesar Augustus. . .."

I started to read, and out of the corner of my eyes, I watched as Mr. Tilley leaned back into his chair and closed his eyes. His body relaxed and his face grew calm; actually, he seemed to become quite peaceful in his chair. He took his hand off the top of his cane. He allowed the cane to lean on the side of his chair and as he sat there with his eyes closed, he folded his hands gently together and held them in his lap. I knew that this was a very special man. A man who knew the word of God, and the hope, joy, and peace that it brings to a person's soul.

I could tell. So far, in my life, I have met quite a few of them.

I read the entire Christmas story from the Gospel of Luke and then I closed the Bible, and I looked up, thinking for a brief moment that the old chap had dozed off, but then I caught my thoughts because I should have known better. His eyes opened and grew wide. The sparkle of the clear blue color of his eyes seemed to reflect the glow of the holiday lights in the room. He smiled, but he did not say a word. I placed the Bible on top of a small end table, reached for a paper that I had written some notes upon for a condensed sermon, and began to speak again.

"Here we are, over two thousand years later and on this special day, we remember and celebrate the birth of a man who never owned more than the clothes on his back, and perhaps, the shoes on his feet. He never wandered more than thirty or so miles from the location where he was born, never spoke on television or radio, never had much more than the words of many mouths to broadcast his message. He influenced a group of people and called them not only his followers but also, he called them his friends. Together with his friends, they walked town-to-town, city-to-city, sleeping on the ground, sleeping in random homes, begging for food and shelter. Yet, his friends followed him, not for money or fame, but because of simple faith in the stories of which he told them. He was indeed, a poor pauper."

Looking up from my paper, my eyes met Mr. Tilley's clear blue eyes, which remained wide, yet he still did not speak to me. He did not even react to my opening words.

I continued to preach, "Yet, this one person has had more impact on the course of history than any other person has. It is a somewhat sad, but true fact that his followers fought many wars for him. There are more songs written, more arguments started and never ended, more love showered down and more words written about him, than any other person who has ever walked God's creation. Yet, I think the one verse that provides more insight about Jesus Christ than any other verse does, are the two lines where they wrote that Jesus wept. He wept when he found out that his friend had died, and he never had the chance to say goodbye to him. That tells me that he knew pain, he knew emotion in his human form, and he walked in the same shoes that we walk in right now. Every day. To me, those words are the most powerful words ever written. They provide me with more hope, joy, and peace, than any other two words could ever convey. My hope and fervent prayer for this Christmas season, is that these words also provide you with the same images, the same joy, and the same comforts, as they do to me. Amen."

Upon my finishing of the mini-sermon, Mr. Tilley leaned forward, while smiling broadly. He once again took his cane in his right hand, picked it up, and waved it symbolically in the air while shouting aloud, "Amen! Thank you, Pastor Paul, for coming here, reading, and preaching to me today. I enjoyed that more than I could ever tell you. You are indeed, a powerful preacher and a man of deep insight and emotion. You kept it brief, not too long and boring and drawn out. I loved it. Fantastic and inspiring thoughts, indeed. May I receive communion too?"

"Of course, Mr. Tilley. I thank you for the compliment,

and I am glad that you enjoyed it. Let us prepare the table of the Lord's Supper together. I will move closer to you. May I use this table?"

He nodded to indicate that I should. While I moved the small end table closer to where he sat, out of the corner of my eye, I noticed the old chap take out a handkerchief from his pants pocket. Mr. Tilley wiped some tears from his eyes as I sat at the table next to him. While I stood up and prepared the sacraments, he assisted me the best that he could.

I spoke the liturgy, and we communed together. After properly packing away communion and returning the end table back to the side of my chair, Mr. Tilley sat back in his chair. I sat in mine and he smiled at me.

"You know that I have not had a Christmas like this in many years, Pastor Paul. A simple visit such as this, well, it frankly, has been marvelous. It is very special for an old cripple such as I am. Do you know why I hobble like this? Are you not curious?"

"I never ask, Mr. Tilley. Each of us has their own crutches, some are obvious, and some are not."

"You are wise beyond your years, young pastor, you really are. I suspect that while you are still very young, you have an extraordinary number of miles under your hood. You have not had it easy either. I can tell because of the look in your eyes. Lots of lingering pain and emotion there. You might be a man of God, but you certainly ain't no patsy ass. What a misconception that is when people think that men and women of faith are lightweights. Indeed, it is actually the opposite! Heard you were quite the professional hockey player at one time and grew up hard and tough. Rough and tumble, New Jersey neighborhoods make men outta boys. No way to avoid it. I imagine ya seen and dealt with quite a bit of, you know what, in your few, short years."

This time, it was my time to smile but to remain quiet.

He pointed with the end of his cane to a picture above the fireplace mantle. I turned, looked, and saw a faded picture of a smiling soldier dressed in what I thought to be a World War Two uniform.

"D Day, Pastor Paul. Omaha Beach. Second Ranger Battalion, United States Army. First wave or thereabouts on the beach. I waded to the shore while being scared shitless. Made it about four hundred feet on the shore and machine gun fire tore my leg and hip to shreds. Wounded but now, pissed off, I crawled along that horrible sand, set up, and fired my rifle and hurled grenades until I passed out from the loss of blood. Horrible, the screams of death all around. Men torn to shreds, pieces of your brothers in arms spitting up and into the air, and showering blood and guts upon you, while you are helpless."

Mr. Tilley lowered his head and stopped speaking for just a moment. It was easy to tell that this was still an incredibly vivid memory in his mind, and quite painful to speak of even all of these years later. He picked up his cane to use it as a prop, as he waved it in the air to depict the impact of the battle.

"Bombs, shells, blinding lights of the explosions of war surround you. You hunker down and pray and your life does indeed flash before your eyes. Death is now commonplace and screams of anguish become somewhat normal. You look up and see the sky full of planes and flashes of light. It looked as if you could jump from wing tip to wing tip because the planes were so close. It is beyond description. Yet, I lived, and others died! Why? They saved my leg and hip, but I never walked correctly ever again. I woke up in a hospital in England. I never slept so damn well, Pastor Paul. To think, I was a championship sprinter in high school, no one could catch me. Now, I walk as if I am an old drunken fool. I know you were a professional athlete. You think you are untouchable. Right? You are invincible! That was the only time that I ever visited the country of France. Guess what? I have no intention of ever returning there."

He waved his cane in the air again, and proclaimed, "Haughty bastards! Don't appreciate the shit that the Brits and we did to save their prissy asses!"

He laughed heartily, and I smiled at him while I said, "Thank you for your service, Mr. Tilley, and for telling me your remarkable story of courage. It is my honor to be in your presence. Do you not have any family left?"

"None, Pastor Paul. Just Jesus, you, and the church. I am gonna leave everything here to Reunion Lutheran Church."

"Why, my goodness, what can I say, except for thank you, Mr. Tilley."

"No need to thank me. It is the right thing to do. Nope, not a single relative left, on either my wife's side or mine. I have outlived them all. My wife, brothers, cousins, nephews and nieces, all of them, now are gone. We were married for sixty years. We had one son, a brave son. He died in combat in the Vietnam War. He served in the United States Army. He was in country one week, one lousy, damn week."

He pointed with his cane again to another picture, also mounted above the fireplace; this picture was a picture of his son. I thought about what a handsome young man he was and how this was such a horrible tragedy.

"I am so sorry, Mr. Tilley. What a terrible loss. What was his name? I would like to include him in my prayers."

The old man now had tears rolling down his cheeks as he struggled to tell me, "James Roger Tilley Junior. Private First Class, J.R. Tilley."

I nodded as I watched the old chap lean forward. His hands shook and quivered while he slowly moved in his chair.

"We have this letter that I keep here in this drawer of this end table here next to this chair. He died about four or five days before Christmas in 1967. I had this letter written for him. I composed the letter to send to him but for obvious reasons, I never did."

Mr. Tilley reached for the handle of a drawer of a small end table next to his chair and opened the drawer. I could see that he carefully and reverently pulled a faded letter out of the drawer, closed it and then opened the letter.

He began to read, "Son, let me tell you first, that your mother and I are prouder of you than words could ever convey. You have been a light to us, a joy in our hearts. I stare at your picture of when you graduated basic training, a soldier, a United States Army Ranger just like your old man. I know right now, the horrors of war have become a reality, but please know that mankind is basically good. I know it is very hard to tell from where you are, but I know it because of what I experienced on a beach we called Omaha in Normandy, France. Righteousness and kindness will always prevail because of God's presence. No matter how dark the days become, know that goodness and kindness will rule. God will not allow anything else. Know that we love you and pray for you every day. Love, your father and your mother."

His voice drifted off as the tears filled his eyes. He extended his hand and motioned for me to grab it. I stood up, walked over, and clasped his hand in mine.

"After he died a hero's death, I tossed away all of my military medals, ribbons, military awards, as well as the ones they shipped home with our son's cold, dead, body. Tossed it all away. It is nuthin' but bullshit to pin medals on our asses, when we left badges of courage, parts of our bodies and our very lives upon the cold ground and inside of coffins. Sacrifice requires no rewards. Only reverence, remembrance, and faith. That will forever be, the only medals we will ever need. Just like Jesus and his medal, I feel it is a mockery. A crown of thorns. Sacrifice is all that we need to recall. Sacrifice in the purest form."

I nodded to indicate my understanding and agreement,

and his grip tightened on my hands.

"Please, Pastor Paul, understand that I am not bitter. Instead, I am glad for the life the good Lord has given me. You see, because of the story you have just read, the words that you just spoke. It is plain to see that Jesus felt the same pain when his best friend died. The same agony that my wife and I felt when our son left this world to be with the Lord. Jesus knew what we feel when we lose special people in our lives. You are quite correct that it is of great comfort. I also know that because of Christmas, the world has hope, joy, and peace. Without it, we have nothing, but with it, we have faith. This old soldier has Christmas faith. Without faith, we are all lost. Faith often is hidden beneath all of what we take for granted. Because of faith, we know that the sun will rise, the sun will set, we will live, and we will die. Faith is the unseen cog that keeps our wheels steady and rolling, without slipping."

Mr. Tilley paused. He still held my hand tightly, and I did not intend to let it go, but he seemed as if he needed to gather his thoughts before he was able to continue.

He spoke again, this time just a little softer, "On a night such as this one, we have to realize that no matter what we face, it is a blessing for all of us to receive the greatest gift of all. The gift of faith. Because of Christmas, there is no gift like it and there never will be, ever again."

Now, some emotions captured him and Mr. Tilley grew louder in voice, "Christmas to me is not about any kind of presents, or Santa Claus, or some stupid, dumb-ass plastic snowmen on my front lawn. What a bunch of bullshit that we give stupid gifts at this time of year because of some sappy story about three wise men!"

I almost laughed aloud at his powerful comments, but I caught the laughter in mid-stream.

"It is about so much more than most people ever could imagine. The light of Heaven entered this world. Perhaps, not on this exact date, but regardless, he arrived, and that is all there is to the whole story. The rest of the holiday foolishness is a bunch of creative, man made nonsense and worthless gobbledygook. Yet, don't get me wrong, I will never stop celebrating Christmas, as long as I draw a breath, or smile a smile. I know my time on this Earth grows short, but I will go with a smile on my face and a Christmas song in my heart. Because of this special night . . . all is well."

He sat back in his chair and smiled as he finally let go of my hand. I turned to walk away, thinking the conversation had now ended and it was time for me to leave. I was wrong. To my surprise, Mr. Tilley became very excited.

"Say, I think we ought to share in a bit of Christmas cheer, Pastor Paul. I have heard that you are a Big Boulder beer man, and I am as you are, where I much prefer Big Boulder to those horribly sweet Dingleberries. This special afternoon, however, I think we need a shot of the high test."

Once again, his cane waving in the air was a directional tool.

"I will direct you to where I keep it in the cupboard, if you would fetch two shot glasses and the bottle for us. I have very much enjoyed this visit. This is a better Christmas than I have had in many a year. Let me tell you, Pastor Paul. Thank you for coming. The least that I can do is to offer you a Christmas toast."

"Well, thank you. However, oh geez, I have two services tonight, Mr. Tilley. I should not. . .."

"Oh, poppycock and horse shit!"

His loud voice startled me a bit, and this time, I could not suppress my laughter. Mr. Tilley laughed along with me.

It was then that I realized that those blue eyes of his were indeed beacons of his spirit. He smoothed the little wisps of white hair on top of his head as if to calm some of his emotions down a bit.

"Do you think Jesus stopped preaching and teaching after he turned the water into wine? After all, the good book tells us that he saved his best for last. Somehow, I know that Martin Luther had a few hits here and there of the good stuff from his wife's special brewery, in order to have the courage to nail that thesis on that church door too. History has lost some of the best parts of that story!"

I thought how this was indeed a very special man. Life's twists, turns and sorrows left him torn, but God kept his spirit and humor alive.

I smiled as Mr. Tilley directed me to where to find the requested "items." I listened carefully, walked into the kitchen, found the glasses and the bottle of whiskey, and returned.

I poured both of us a shot and Mr. Tilley struggled to steady himself upon his feet. He leaned upon his cane as I reached out and steadied him with my arm. Once he was upright, and not wavering, we lifted the glasses in a toast.

"Here is to Christmas, Pastor Paul. Christmas faith. May the joy of Christmas and the real message never leave our hearts! You see, we have nothing really to hang our hats on to nail down this Christmas story. Some gospels do not even mention it. We only believe because we have the gift of faith. Faith at Christmas time is very different, pastor. Each year, it inspires me to keep going for another year. Have to say that it kinda winds me up. Someday, the wind-up crank will not work, and I will go to meet the Lord with a smile on my face and faith in my heart. Faith. Christmas faith . . . it keeps me upright and moving ahead. Cheers."

We swigged the two shots down.

After some additional small talk, I left him with a prayer or two, a handshake, a hug, and a wish for a happy Christmas. I still had plenty of time to arrive home and spend some time with my wife and children before the Christmas Eve worship services started this evening.

It had all worked out fabulously.

I placed my Bible and the communion kit into the back seat of the jeep, jumped in, started the engine, and backed out slowly from his driveway. During the entire return ride home, back to the parsonage at Reunion Lutheran Church, I had a nagging thought to record some of my ideas that I took away from this afternoon's special meeting.

Upon my arrival home at the parsonage, I greeted my dear wife; I told her of my visit with Mr. Tilley over some hot tea, and then chatted up a storm with the children. They were very excited with the imminent arrival of Christmas, and as all young children tend to do, they bounced off a wall or two.

Binky had the children baking Christmas cookies and Heather Sarah was mixing her first batch of fudge. I am not sure that she did not have more on the end of her nose than she did in the bowl.

Nonetheless, she was mixing fudge!

I stood in the doorway watching and laughing at the scene, when suddenly the final parts of the fragmented thoughts, of which I had formed upon leaving Mr. Tilley's house, came rushing into my mind. I excused myself, walked into the living room, and sat at a small desk we kept in the corner of the room.

A small, expiring fire was struggling valiantly to stay alive in the fireplace. I would eventually toss a log or two upon it, but for now, I needed to complete my writing mission. The Christmas tree glowed in the background and cast some colored reflections upon my paper. I picked up my pencil, grabbed a piece of paper, and wrote down my thoughts. The thoughts came quickly, and I felt as if my maturity in my writings was now evolving for the better. I no longer created sprawling and rambling sermons or other drivel in my other compositions, nor attempted to create glowing words of inspiration and praise with fillers. Nowadays, I tend to write shorter and more concise.

"Faith at Christmas time is special; it is very different

from faith at other times of the year. It keeps old soldiers upright and allows them to drown out the horrors of war. Christmas faith calms the heartbreak of lost loved ones, and it brings joy to memories of the good times as well as the times yet to come. Without faith, we have nothing. It is the unseen light, which guides us all. It is the beacon in amidst of turmoil, and at Christmas, it steered not only wise kings from foreign lands, but it also guided lowly shepherds in the fields, as well as faithful parishioners heading to worship on Christmas Eve. I think faith at Christmas time is the most powerful tool we can possess, in order to continue to charge ahead through life's battles unscathed for another year. It represents the pinnacle of God's love and glory."

When I placed my pencil down, I noticed that snow had started to fall and looking out towards the church, I could see the tiny webs of the snowflakes gathering along the window sills and ledges of the parsonage's windows.

It was a very fitting setting for Christmas Eve.

I heard our daughter calling for me from the kitchen to come and see her fudge, and I gathered up my notes and placed them in my pocket. I would work it into the sermon tonight; somehow, I knew that I would.

Gifts at Christmas time were never the same for me after that wonderful visit on Christmas Eve with Mr. Tilley. The good Lord will forgive me, but despite the honor and love of which we give Christmas gifts to each other, somehow for me, deep in the back of my mind, they always had that now famous, Mr. Tilley "bullshit" tag hung upon them.

From thereon in, I always thought that every gift played a secondary role to having received the thoughtful gift of Christmas faith. Mr. Tilley had taught me more about Christmas in a few hours than years of seminary and being a pastor, could ever teach me.

Mr. Tilley had taught me about the best gift ever given when he taught me about an old soldier's Christmas faith.

I presided over his funeral a few years later. Ironically and profoundly, perhaps even predictably; he passed away on Christmas Day.

In retrospect, though, maybe irony and the other elements of life had nothing at all to do with it.

I think it was really all about faith.

THE END

Where the Cold Wind Whistles

It was late in the afternoon on Christmas Eve, and the cold wind whistled at the eaves of the old house. It whipped across the porch of the house, gaining velocity as it tore at the balusters and chased a small dusting of snow across the weathered floorboards of the porch. The windows along the front of the house rattled and shook, while the wind made its way across the wooden surface of the porch, moving as if it were a freight train rolling down the tracks.

Yet, as cold as the wind was outside on this late afternoon, where the colder wind was whistling, was actually inside of the home.

It was a small home, only nine-hundred square feet or thereabouts, built somewhere in the late 1930s. The first floor consisted of a living room with a fireplace, a small dining nook, of which could barely contain a table for two persons to sit at, and a kitchen with a small back porch off the rear of the kitchen.

Perhaps, the most striking feature of the home, other than the long front porch and the magnificent fireplace, would be a long, oak-railed, hardwood staircase that led to the upstairs where the only bathroom in the home was, as well as two bedrooms located on the second floor. A small backyard in the rear of the home, a small side yard, a gravel driveway, and that was about all there was to this humble abode.

The home was located in rural New Jersey, in Sussex

County, and it sat on a sharp and somewhat dangerous turn of a country road. It sat amongst what were once dairy farms with open cow pastures, and within the boundaries of a town that seemed as if most people had even forgotten that it existed.

The cold wind, however, had not forgotten, and it whistled out of the north while bringing with it a Christmas chill that rarely, if ever, felt colder than it would feel on this Christmas Eve. It froze every ounce of moisture it touched, turning the gravel in the driveway of the old home into a frozen landscape, of which will not loosen until the warmer and gentler winds of April arrived from the south. The snow spitting out of the overcast sky settled in small dusty circles, chasing in the wind as if it were a sprinkling of talcum powder upon the frozen surfaces.

Inside the home, an old man slowly shuffled towards a teakettle that was sitting on a burner on the oven. The kettle was screaming out into the air, spewing a small puff of steam from out of its porcelain whistler, signifying that the water inside was now boiling over. He reached for the knob on the oven, turned the flame off, and pulled the teakettle from the burner. A waiting teacup contained a lone tea bag, waiting for the boil of the water to drown it. A douse of water, a slow steep, a wave or two of the string and the comforting aroma of warm tea drifted in the air of the kitchen.

The old man slowly shuffled back to his chair in the living room, a chair positioned right next to the fireplace, the chair legs rubbing against the stone hearth. The fireplace, which now softly crackled with some hardwoods, glowed and smoldered in front of the old man. Inside of the fireplace, the hardwoods succumbed to the heat and flames, and they were now about to leave this world, just as we all will someday, as ashes and dust.

The fire was low; it was ready for another log, but the old man had set his mind to sipping warm tea before he ventured out to the porch to pick out another log. He needed the warmth of the tea to ward off where the cold wind whistled.

You see, the cold wind also whistled in the old man's heart on this dark, dreary Christmas Eve.

He sat in the chair, cupping the teacup tightly with his hands, desperately trying to capture some warmth from the cup. Warmth, which did very little to offset the pain of the arthritis in his fingers, pain gained from a lifetime of hard work, and warmth that did very little to chase away the cold wind from his heart.

An old, vacuum tube radio sat on a table, it crackled with the sounds of a local radio station playing an endless string of the same, old, Christmas tunes, droning on and on endlessly with versions of the same songs he had heard a few thousand times before. The radio proudly sat upon an old oak table, with the happy glow of the tubes inside illuminating the wall behind the radio. The old man always thought how at least, the old radio provided some elements of warmth from the array of vacuum tubes glowing inside. If he reached deep in his pockets and finally bought one of those newfangled solid-state radios, he thought how he would miss the glow of those tubes.

Simple warmth projected, and it brought some type of roundabout comfort to the old man.

The old man owned very few items that were new or modern because he much preferred the old things in which he had.

After all, he paid for them all, and in his opinion; they were a lot better than anything new in which he could purchase. He owed no one anything, and he felt as if the world owed him very little in return.

While he sat there in his chair, sipping his tea, he suddenly thought that he heard the scamper of little feet and that he caught the blur of a quick dash of an annoying field mouse scurrying across his living room. However, his eyes were not quite as sharp as they once were, and his ears were not tuned too well either. He thought, how since he lost his faithful house cat, a few months back; the field mice had become quite a bit braver. His cat, "Pumpkin" was not only a faithful companion, but she was quite the capable hunter too! She was a mouse policewoman.

The old man leaned back into his chair and sighed a bit because he was now so alone. Even his old cat was gone.

He had seen many a Christmas Eve, and many a Christmas Day, come and go during his lifetime. Some were fun, some were sad, and as of late, most of them were forgettable.

They all were a blur now, and in reality, the holiday now meant very little to him.

It was just another marker in time, a passing fancy, a day of which he knew to some, was very joyous, yet to him, it was just another cup of tea or two, a hot bowl of soup, a nip or two of whiskey, some old songs on the radio and it would be over again for another year.

Perhaps he would see another Christmas, then again, maybe not. He did not actually care, or think about it. Every day was pretty much the same to the old man.

His extent of decorating for Christmas these days was a wreath upon his front door, and a small, ceramic Christmas tree that he had for years and years. The tree was about a foot or so tall, with plastic lights on the tips of the edges of the molded branches, lights that were cast in various colors to glow very softly into the night. This was the type of little decoration, which you sat neatly upon a tabletop; it was unobtrusive, to say the least. It had one little light bulb to maintain, and the old man plugged it in every night during the holiday season to enjoy the glow. Simple, easy and carefree. When the holiday was over, the old man put the tree in a little box and set it in his basement on a shelf, along with a lot of other memories. His entire life had now become a shelf of memories.

He thought perhaps that his wife had purchased the little tree so long ago, but now, he just was not too sure where it had come from. Who knows, or in fact, who really cares? That was the root of his trouble. He felt as if no one really cared.

His wife had been gone now for over fifteen years, and she too was now just a memory in his heart.

A heart where the cold wind whistled.

They were married over fifty years, only had one child, a beautiful girl who grew into a gorgeous woman. A woman who lost a brave battle with breast cancer a few years ago. Everyone went too soon, all of his loved ones.

Gone off to a place where the cold wind whistles.

The pain of Christmas often exceeds the magic of the holiday. The smiles of Christmas morning, years down the road fade, and turn into despair. The holiday of joy turns into the holiday of dread, and the ghosts of Christmas in the past chase loneliness into many, many lonely hearts.

The old man glanced at the fire. The dying embers required another log, and his tea was almost gone now. He pushed off on the arms of the chair, his body aching and protesting, leaving the comfort of the folds of the old chair. He swigged the last drop of tea and slowly shuffled his way towards the kitchen.

A stop by the sink to drop his cup in the dishpan caused a pause at the kitchen window, where the old man stared out into a stark, white landscape. The snow was now coming down hard and steady, and it grew deeper in his backyard. The old man thought how perfect it was for a nice, white coating of snow to filter down upon Christmas Eve.

It certainly set a mood if he felt as if he had a mood to set.

He had seen many a white Christmas Eve and Christmas Day; this was just a passing fancy for a moment or two.

"Let it snow," he spoke aloud. He did not care about the

snowstorm. He had no plans to travel anywhere; he had plenty of milk, bread, eggs and such in the refrigerator, and many cans of soup and other foods stored in his cupboards. He also had plenty of wood for his fireplace.

He just needed another log for his fire and he knew when he reached for a log from his stockpile on the porch, he would disturb another nest of field mice, and they would scurry out of the wood and dash in all directions. He was not too sure why the mice annoyed him so very much, or perhaps they did not annoy him as much as they reminded him of the loss of his faithful feline companion. As he shuffled off in the direction of the back porch, he thought how maybe, just maybe, he really did need another cat to chase the field mice away. The snap of those traps in the middle of the night always were a bit of a disturbing sound.

Maybe. . ..

The old man opened the door to the back porch, leaned into the pile of hardwoods stacked in a long, neat pile and picked two or three logs from the top of the pile. He ignored the mice scurrying about and tucked the logs under his arm. He was old, but still strong and sturdy. Once he got his bearings and feet underneath him, that is. He made his way back to the fireplace, placed the logs upon the fire and in just a few minutes, once the smoke of a dash or two of moisture left the wood and escaped up the chimney, his fire restored to the mission of attempting to chase away the locations where the cold wind whistled.

The fire could reach and warm many spaces and chase away the cold, however, it could not reach inside the old man's heart.

The old table radio crackled a bit. The old man walked over, and he fiddled with the tuning knob to fine tune the frequency just a little. A careful and slow adjustment of the knob did the trick. The magic of the radio waves restored and the music came booming in.

"Hmm, the snow is changing the signals as the nighttime approaches," the old man said aloud to the walls and the cold wind.

When he turned to walk back to his chair and the comfort of the fire, to his complete surprise; there was a loud and somewhat frantic knock at his front door. He stood for just a moment because the shock of actually having a knock at his front door had overcome him. Other than the occasional and very rare knock from the postman, in order to signal a letter or other delivery of some significance, no one, and that truly meant no one, ever knocked at his front door or visited the old man.

Now on a late afternoon, which was quickly turning into an early evening on Christmas Eve, in the midst of a snowstorm, there came a mysterious knock at his door.

Who could this be?

He could never even imagine!

After a pause or two, he overcame his shock and he rather hastily made his way towards the front door. Something deep inside of him told him that this visitor or visitors were in some need of aid.

After all, Christmas Eve, snowstorms, knocks at the front door. There must be some type of significant purpose behind this visit.

He peered out the window of his living room that faced the porch and the front yard of his home, but he could not see anything. It was snowing so hard now, and growing darker and darker. Therefore, he was not at all surprised when nothing was visible. He reached the door, turned the knob, and flung the door open. The cold wind whistled in, taking over the precious heat and along with its cold and somewhat cruel intentions, it delivered a few snowflakes into the front hallway of the old man's house.

There in front of the old man, shivering a bit in the cold and snow . . . was a young woman. She was tightly holding very close to her, a little girl. They were dressed in light jackets, they wore no hats, nor were they equipped with scarves or other clothing with which to confront the cold. You could see rather quickly that they were not dressed in a manner of which would significantly ward off where the cold wind would whistle with such a wintery onslaught.

Without any hesitation, the old man sensed that this was an emergency situation, which had arrived at his front door. He felt no need to be apprehensive; he knew in his heart that there was a good reason, for these people dressed as they were, to be calling upon him. In addition, there still remain some kind and gentle souls in this world who have no ill intentions.

"Please, please! Come in! Come in! It is too cold outside and you are not dressed for such a night as we are going to experience this evening," the old man called out, almost pleading with them as he waved them into his home.

The young woman smiled, she tugged at the young girl and she too, without hesitation, stepped into the warmth of the old man's home.

Once inside the entrance of the home, the young woman looked up at the old man and explained, "Oh, thank you, sir. Thank you, for your kindness! Our car broke down at the base of your driveway. We slid on the snow on that tricky turn and the front tire of the car seems to have broken off, or we are now just hopelessly stuck. I am so sorry to disturb you, but we were cutting across the county and I knew this road would bring us to the highway. We saw your lights and smelled the smoke from your fire. Please, could we use your telephone to call my husband?"

The old man nodded, and he waved towards the kitchen, while saying, "You are not the first car that has slid on that turn in a snowstorm. I have lived here for over sixty years and let me tell you that there have been a few too many! Please, please come inside. You look so cold."

The old man provided a hint of advice and wisdom as he added, "In this type of weather, always keep heavier clothes and coats on hand just in case of emergencies on the road."

The old man spoke from experience. He had broken down on a road or two, or three, in his time too. He hustled them inside the home, and the two of them were very anxious to come inside, where it was warm and out of the harsh weather.

"Of course, you may use my telephone. It is right here on the wall in the kitchen."

He pointed the way to the kitchen, and they followed him.

"Please, young lady, take your jacket off, shake off the snow and ice and sit in the chair next to my fireplace. Please go, sit and warm up, while your mother makes the telephone call."

The old man suddenly felt alive, he felt a purpose in his life, and he happily moved into action. Even his aches and pains left his old bones. He waved his hands to direct the mother and her daughter into the different locations. When he watched the young girl nod her head and eagerly dash into the living room to sit in front of the warm fireplace, the old man was satisfied.

He now directed his attention to the child's mother. She had found the telephone, dialed the number, and she now appeared as if she was speaking to her husband on the telephone.

The old man stood and listened.

"Yes, yes, we are warm and safe now. I am sorry about the car, but I hit some snow or a patch of ice. . .."

She paused for a time in order to listen to what appeared to be a lecture from her husband on the other end.

"I know. I admit that I do drive too fast. This kind man has allowed us to use his telephone and Amanda is sitting in front of his fireplace now. The address? Oh yes, we are in Newton. At least I think that we are in Newton. Please, hang on and I will find out."

She held the receiver up in the air so that her husband might be able to hear the answer and capture the directions. She turned towards the old man and asked, "Sir, please your address."

"Why yes, it is in Newton and it is directly off of Henry Farm Road. Two turns past the gas station and then one long left. Number four, Henry Farm Road. The only mailbox and a house for two miles once you make the turn. I will make sure the porch lights are on as a guiding light in the snow."

"Did you hear that, honey? Yes, you are correct, number four Henry Farm Road . . . yes, yes, that is what he said. Two turns past the gas station. Okay, okay, yes."

The old man stood, and he continued to listen, then he watched and he smiled when he saw that the young mother seemed more relaxed, she nodded, listened to her husband's continued response, and then she hung up the telephone with a poignant, "I love you. Thank you and please be careful."

The young mother turned and smiled while saying, "Thank you so much, sir. You have been more than kind. I do not know what we would have done without you! There is not another house for miles, and we are indeed, underdressed. I have learned my lesson for winter travel."

She chuckled a bit at the thought of her hard-earned lesson and thought about how she was long overdue to introduce herself to this total stranger. A stranger who has been more than kind to admit them to his home on such a brutally cold day. She extended her hand to introduce herself and greet the old man.

"Hello, my name is Marilyn Scott, and our daughter's name is Amanda."

The old man now leaned upon the counter in the kitchen. His exuberance at the onset of the emergency had caused his energy to peak and he now relaxed.

With the relaxation, his aches and pains returned.

He held his hand out and with a gentle smile, the old man said, "Hello. It is my pleasure to meet you, Marilyn. I am Harold Jenkins, and please do call me, Harold. Is your husband on the way?"

"Nice to meet you, Harold, and thank you so much. Yes, he has to come over Hamburg Mountain, though. He had to work late on Christmas Eve and he works downstate. He has a big truck though with four-wheel drive and he will be fine."

Marilyn smiled and laughed gently while she waved her hands in the air and frankly stated, "Luckily, he is a better driver in the snow than I proved to be!"

Harold did not comment, but he looked at the young woman, studied her, and he sensed that she still had a chill upon her.

"Let me turn the porch lights on for your husband to guide him along and to see in the snow. Would you like some warm tea? Does Amanda enjoy hot cocoa? I can prepare us all some warm drinks."

"Yes! Oh, thank you. That would be wonderful."

"Please go near the fire and check on Amanda. First, I will go and turn the lights on, and then, I will bring our warm drinks into the living room very shortly."

Harold waved towards the living room; Marilyn nodded and headed off to check on her daughter and to warm her bones by the fire. In short order, Harold turned the porch lights on, he prepared the drinks and he shuffled around from cupboard-to-cupboard, while searching for a serving tray, he knew he had somewhere in the dark confines of one of these cabinets. It had been a very long time since Mr. Harold Jenkins had visitors on Christmas Eve, and the least he could do was try to be a cordial host to these poor people stranded in a snowbank. After a number of misses, Harold found the tray; he dusted it off with a towel, placed the drinks upon it, along with some cream and sugar, and carefully carried the tray and refreshments into the living room.

"Here you go, Amanda. Some hot cocoa to help warm you, and Marilyn, for you, a nice cup of tea. I have cream here in the little cup and some sugar if you prefer those. I just take a dash of both."

Amanda jumped up. She glanced at her mother, and she looked for confirmation of what she was about to say. It was obvious that Marilyn had coached her daughter on the conversation.

"Thank you, Mr. Jenkins, for allowing us to come in and get so warm in front of your fire and for the cocoa. You are a very kind man to help us out like this."

The little girl glanced back towards her mother, who smiled and nodded to her to confirm that she had delivered her speech correctly.

Harold Jenkins looked down on the little girl, he guessed her to be eight or nine years of age, she had green eyes with a sparkle of the fireplace in them, curly black hair, and she was wearing a Christmas sweater with reindeer and snowmen dancing upon it.

His old heart melted, and suddenly, the spot where the cold wind whistles had to find another place of which to torture.

His small act of kindness, bestowed upon his stranded guests, had warmed his heart and his soul.

Because of the wide smile and sincerity of the little girl, the old man stumbled a bit on his response, but he found his words and he recovered.

Harold steadied himself with a shuffle of his feet, leaned over, and said, "Thank you, Amanda. I very seldom have anyone come by here, and I must say that although it is under difficult circumstances that you are here, and I am sorry about your car, it has done me a world of good to have, unexpected, or otherwise . . . well, just to have guests here on Christmas Eve."

"Are you alone here, Harold?" Marilyn asked.

"Yes, my wife passed away many years ago, and our daughter has been gone now too for a number of years. I am very old, and when you live to an old age, you tend to outlive your loved ones."

His profound, yet factual statement caused Harold some emotion, and for just a few brief moments, the old man felt that he had to fight back on some tears. He quickly looked away from his two unexpected guests and then recovered with a slight change of subjects.

"Until July of this year, I had my old orange tabby cat, Pumpkin, to keep me company. She passed away now too, and I miss her greatly. Now, the field mice have the run of this old home. Pumpkin kept them away, but now there are so many holes in this old house and December has been so cold, the mice have decided to move in with me too!"

They at first shared an exchange of condolences at Harold's losses and then the conversation turned to a laugh or two at the new squatters of Harold's home.

Amanda continued to tell Harold all about her own cat, a female named, of course, as so many other little girls tend to name their pet felines, "Whiskers." She excitedly rambled on and on about her cat, while Harold listened carefully and patiently to her description and he, too, felt her love.

After a few sips of hot cocoa, Amanda ran off to study, with a little girl curiosity, the old home. Amongst warnings from her mother, of, "Please do not touch anything," Amanda nodded and wandered with wide-eyed Christmas Eve wonder. First, she found the old table radio proudly playing Christmas music, then she dashed off to the little Christmas tree, and then off to study all other items of fascination to a little girl of her age. The old home was somewhat of a museum to her, and Amanda ran from object-to-object, with her mother gently warning again for her not to touch anything or break anything.

"This is such a grand old home, Harold, it is

marvelous." Marilyn admired the house as she studied the living room. "I would love to have a house like this someday. Right now, we rent a small house because it is all we can afford right now. It is so expensive. We are saving our pennies, and I do mean saving penny-by-penny, for a down payment on a home."

Harold nodded and mumbled, "Thank you for the compliment. It is an old home, but it is indeed, grand. I can only imagine how difficult it is for young people these days."

When Amanda found Harold's dusty old checkerboard tucked on a table in a dark corner of the living room, she squealed with glee and loudly asked, "Can we play a game of checkers, Mr. Jenkins? I love checkers! I always beat Daddy at checkers."

Harold smiled and waved for her to bring it over to his chair, and he warned Amanda, "Of course, we can play a game or two; however, I will warn you that I just might be the best checker player in the entire world."

And play they did, in front of the fireplace, listening to Christmas music, with the glow of the old ceramic Christmas tree dimly lit on a table, as they passed the time.

Harold won a game or two, and then it seemed as if he let his guard down on purpose, and allowed Amanda a few wins too.

They laughed, and they conversed for what seemed as if it were hours, until a knock at the door signaled the arrival of Mr. Scott.

"Daddy is here!" Amanda shouted as they made their way to the front door. To find that indeed, Mr. Scott had arrived safely, to pick up his precious wife and daughter. After a tearful reunion, Marilyn introduced her husband to Mr. Harold Jenkins.

The two men shook hands, and Mr. Scott said, "Merry Christmas, Harold. Thank you for your kindness, and for rescuing the two people most precious to me in this entire world."

"Oh, it was nothing. It is a terrible night out there. You should be careful now, leave the car there, it will be fine. The town plows seldom go down this road. An old farmer, who lives up the road apiece, will eventually plow us out with his tractor. I will give him a call to warn him about the car. We can pull it out when the weather breaks. I will keep an eye on it. That turn is terrible out there. It is not the first car stuck in those snow banks there, and I am sure it will not be the last one."

All too soon, it was time for goodbye. When Marilyn hugged and gave Harold a kiss on his cheek, while Amanda gave him a hug around his waist, the cold wind left the old man's heart forever.

They left with a promise to stay in touch, an exchange of telephone numbers, and a statement always to remain friends.

Harold stood on the old porch and watched, then waved as they jumped in the truck and made their way down the driveway and out on the main road. The snow was deep, but Mr. Scott had a formidable truck with which to make their way safely along.

When the old man returned to his chair, he gently replaced the checkerboard to the dark corner of the room and he sat once again in front of the warmth of the fireplace.

Harold Jenkins now had considerable tears in his eyes, yet he had joy upon his heart. . ..

Christmas Day came and went.

The next day or so after Christmas, Harold helped Mr. Scott in pulling the trapped car out of that tricky snow bank, and as a reward for his kindness, Harold was the lucky recipient of some home-baked Christmas cookies, and a home-baked mince pie too! Everything delivered in thanks for Harold's kindness.

All too soon, Christmas week was a memory. New

Year's Day came, and it was soon past too.

Snow came down and snow melted.

One late March day, Harold was in the kitchen when the telephone rang. He was happy to speak once again with Marilyn Scott, who after some pleasant exchanges and general chit chat asked Harold if they might come over for a visit.

"Of course, of course. I will get the checkerboard out," Harold replied, thrilled at the prospect of a visit from his new friends. Around an hour later, a knock at the door confirmed his visitor's arrival. Harold eagerly shuffled to the door, and his surprise at the sight now in front of him was somewhat hard to hide. The Scott family stood there smiling, and Amanda held a cardboard box in her little hands. While under the careful watch of her father, she tried very hard to keep a little kitten from escaping the confines of the cardboard container.

"Whiskers had kittens, Mr. Jenkins! And we brought you an orange one! The kitten is the same color that you told us Pumpkin's color was!"

Harold reached over and pulled the little kitten out of the box and with a wide smile; he knew it was just what he needed.

Those annoying mice will never stand a chance now.

Harold could not contain his joy.

"Oh my! What a little cutie she is! And look how smart, she is already looking around the room for mice. Thank you! Thank you! You know, I think that I will name her, Pumpkin."

Harold Jenkins was never alone again. Between his new mouse policewoman on duty, and the Scott family, they all made sure of that fact.

He lived to the ripe old age of ninety-eight and when he passed away, having no living relatives, he left everything to the Scott family. He left them the house, the property, the old pickup truck, the radio, the ceramic Christmas tree, the checkerboard, all of it, and Pumpkin the cat too.

The Scott family moved into the old home. They fixed it up as their money allowed them to, and made it into a grand showplace.

Amanda Scott grew up there and that wonderful, little girl grew up to be a lovely, gorgeous woman, with a kind heart and a gentle soul.

One magnificent day, far into the future, on a wonderful May day, with crisp golden sunshine and a warm spring breeze that captured the scent of the blooms of spring flowers, Miss Amanda Scott, dressed as the most gorgeous bride a man could ever imagine, strolled down that wonderful, oak staircase. She walked gracefully across the floor with joy in her heart and love within her soul as she made her way over to her groom. There was joy in the old house on this magnificent day, as Amanda married the love of her life, right in front of that fireplace in the old home.

A place where Harold Jenkins looked down upon from his lofty perch and smiled because he knew it was the place where the cold wind used to whistle.

You see, as strong and as cold as that wind could whistle, in the long haul of life, when confronted with love, it never really stood much of a chance.

THE END

The Radio

Chapter 1

A Special Gift

"Yeah, yeah, yeah, I like this kinda aftershave lotion, there, honey. Let's see, yeah, yeah, yeah, skin attacker. That's the kind of stuff that I like. The stuff in the blue bottle with the horse's head on the front. It smells sorta like the stale beer in the bottom of the bottles. Ya know, the beer that I save for Pussface the cat to drink."

My dear Mum screwed her face up at the old man's description of her Christmas present to our father. My sister, Dottie, looked at me, and I shrugged my shoulders. It was actually difficult to tell if that meant he liked the scent or not. Because I was an annoying and somewhat dopey kid, and even at the young age of twelve or thereabouts, always needed to inject logic into situations, I ventured deeper into the description waters.

"Does it smell like Dingleberry beer or does it smell like Big Boulder beer, Dad?"

Without a moment of hesitation, the old man answered, "Ah shit, those damn Dingleberries are way too sweet! I can't figah out how Ronzo sucks 'em down. Nah, nah, nah, this stuff is the high test. It definitely smells like stale, Big Boulder!"

After overlooking the old man's colorful language on a Christmas Day, Mum smiled. I think she felt some type of redemption that her aftershave selection had made the cut after all.

Here we were, the entire Henson family, gathered in the living room at our family home, located at 182 Belmont

Avenue in Haledon, New Jersey. We gathered for our annual Christmas morning festival of tearing apart wrapping paper and bows while happily tossing the spent decorations all over the floor. There we sat, with Christmas music playing on A.M. radio station WPAT, all tucked underneath the glow of a fake Christmas tree, (we had a real Christmas tree one year, and that adventure I will leave for another story) all in the pursuit of good tidings of comfort and joy.

The peace on Earth and good will toward men phase of this Christmas Day was currently in limbo, and the level of goodwill and peace invoked upon mankind, was entirely dependent upon the amount of Big Boulder beer that the old man and my grandfather would consume.

We were now well into the Christmas gift giving phase of this operation, and Mum worked hard to gather up spent wrapping paper, ribbons, gift tags and bows, while the packages were torn apart, and we tossed it all aside and much to the chagrin of Mum, all over the room. We looked as if we were a bunch of hound dogs digging up buried bones.

Mum always fretted about her housekeeping and this type of operation was the epitome of production of those pesky, as she called them, "Bits and bobs, and fuds" that littered the rug of our living room and tracked throughout the house for days on end. When you add the occasional plastic needle that fell off the tree, and you found it on the kitchen floor in July, then this entire operation was a nightmare for our mother. Mum would lie awake at night for hours, resisting the urge to break out the vacuum and patrol for errant Christmas tree needles and the occasional gathering of fuds.

"Didn't I get a brandy-dandy-fancy New York Bugs hat this year? The old hat is kinda greasy. I was lookin' for a new kinda hat, ya know, the one they wear at a home game, with the white pinstripes," the old man bantered as he scoured his remaining packages on "his side" of the Christmas tree for a telltale package in the shape of a baseball hat. The old man already had about five New York Bug hats.

Our mother always arranged the individual piles of presents under the Christmas tree on Christmas Eve, into neat piles grouped by each family member. It was always part of Henson family Christmas etiquette to respect each other's boundaries and always wait your "turn" to open a present.

"Wait, wait, wait, geez, will ya wait, kids! Geez, the presents ain't gonna go anywhere. I think it is your mother's turn. Go ahead, honey and open one."

"I think it is Paulie's turn," our dear mother commented.

"Nah, nah, nah! JUST GO WILL YA!" The old man was ready to skip the good tidings portion of this process now, too. "Open that one!" The old man pointed at a small package tucked deep under the tree. Mum grabbed it, tore it open, and carefully placed the wrapping paper in a brown trash bag.

"Oh my. Perfume."

The old man smiled and winked at Mum.

"Yeah, yeah, yeah, the guys in the shop told me it is the kind that smells sort of like an old wine cork, after it has been in the garbage bin for a day or so. Ya know . . . it smells like one of those peanut-new-oars wines." My father did not quite get the pronunciation correct, but he came close enough for us to figure it out.

"That's nice, dear. Thank you."

Mum placed the perfume aside.

The Christmas package opening went on for a little while longer. Our family did not have a ton of extra money, but our dear Mum was a gold medal and red-carpet member of the local Christmas club at the First National Bank and Trust Company up the street from us on Belmont Avenue.

Mum would faithfully deposit hard-earned coins beginning next week to prepare for next Christmas. In addition, the old man was one of the world's hardest workers.

Our parents were exceptionally good to us and we lived as honestly, and as well as we could, while still considering our means. Our parents did not incur mountains of debt for the sake of Christmas joy. Times were much different back then. We would receive a number of practical gifts for Christmas, a few lower budget gifts, and we would each receive one large and more expensive gift. That gift was highly touted and advertised by Mum and the old man as a "special gift."

Here we go now into the meat and potatoes of the stash! A few rock-and-roll records for Dottie, the obligatory socks, and underwear for each family member. A Substantial Industries wrench for the old man, with an extension to reach that one stubborn bolt, on our 1964 Putter Classic Model 200 family car that always comes loose and causes some kind of rattle under the floorboards. A pack of hockey trading cards for me, along with a new mouth guard. I played the position of goalie in hockey, so my parents were trying hard to preserve a few of my teeth. A bone for Skippy the terrier, a new (actually it was a used dish from the local thrift store) dish for Pussface the cat for his stale beer, a potholder for Mum, and finally, the new baseball cap of his favorite team for the old man.

Our grandfather, who was Mum's father, or as we called him, "Gramps," always stayed up late at night, he slept in later in the morning, and he would come down later from his apartment on the second floor of our house and join us for Christmas tea. He would open his Christmas gifts at the kitchen table; therefore, he did not have to experience this long, annual Henson ritual of joyful gift giving. We already knew that he was receiving his English toffee hard candies, some special English tea and underwear.

Fritzie, our sometimes-wayward and often abusive parakeet, managed to eke out one of those seed whoosies that you clip to the side of the birdcage. By this afternoon, he will have torn it off the side of the cage and he would be tossing it around the bottom of the cage. The old man would have to endure a beak attack (or wear his work gloves) to reach in the cage and extract it. It was worth it to risk the seed whoosie type of gift this year, because last Christmas, Mum gave him a new ding-a-ling bell, which he rang every four seconds for a week straight, until the old man tore it off the cage and threw it away.

It was now down to the grand finale, the last "special" gifts for my sister and me. This did not count the smaller gifts, which we would receive tomorrow on Mum's English holiday of Boxing Day. Those were usually special foods, candy, or the occasional surprise gift of larger significance. Kids in our neighborhood who called Boxing Day by the usual New Jersey term of "the day after Christmas" called these types of gifts, stocking stuffers.

"Okay, here you go, Dorothy. Here is your last gift. A special one," the old man said as he reached behind the tree to a secret compartment deep within the confines of Christmas magic, and he pulled out a large present and handed it to my sister. "I hope you like it. We had to go all over the damn place to find it. Wait 'till ya hear how I finally got it!"

As far as the old man was concerned, the prerequisite for the "special gift" always included some long and drawn-out tale of how he would seek out and finally purchase the coveted special gift. The old man generally broadcasted these stories, sometimes with an icepack on his forehead, later in the day on Christmas Day, very late in the day on Boxing Day or during Christmas week, when relatives would stop by and visit us. The slightly embellished stories, laced with the old man's colorful language and authentic northern New Jersey accent, always popped up after vast quantities of Big Boulder beer floated in the old man's bloodstream. These stories included riding for miles and miles over treacherous icy roads, and navigating through blinding blizzards, in his beloved 1964 Putter Classic Model 200 car, in order to find a store on the outskirts of East Jacuzzi, New Jersey.

One particularly dramatic and beer-filled Christmas. The old man tried to sell our Uncle Ed on a story, which included that he rented a dog sled from a New Jersey Eskimo, in order to make it over the hill and dale.

Anyway, there in the store, the old man often resorted to hand-to-hand combat with four-hundred-pound hulking bruisers or faced a team of ninja warriors as he tried to procure the coveted prize. One year, he had to avoid fire-breathing dragons and bear traps, in order to purchase the last remaining "special gift" known to exist on the face of the Earth.

My sister was three years older than I was, and she now was well into the rebellious phase of her teenage years. She usually would snap back to the old man on a comment such as that one, and complain that she did not want to hear another tale of precarious Christmas gift procurement, but since it was Christmas, she decided to cut him a break. She knew the item, which she requested for Christmas since early in April of this year, was as commonplace as the beer in our refrigerator was.

Because we were inherently evil and despicable kids, one day, when the old man and Mum went out food shopping, we had already snooped in our stash of Christmas packages. During our evil reconnaissance mission, Dorothy confirmed the special gift to be a strawberry-colored curling iron and matching strawberry and orange hair dryer, autographed by the famous singer and movie star Crystal Zirconium. She now had to whip up some fake surprise faces, in addition to some phony shock and awe when she opened the gift. The pressure was on her now, but I had confidence in her ability to pull it off.

I ran into a bit of trouble during my annual snooping mission as Mum tricked me and she wrapped the special gift in double layers of wrapping paper. Just to further thwart my covert efforts, Mum picked out wrapping paper for my gift, which even when you pressed down hard on the paper to try to look at the writing on the box, while you held it up in a bright light, I still could not read the letters underneath the paper.

The box was perfectly square, not too big, but it was too small to be hockey related. The only faint clue was a gentle rattle of what sounded as if they were loose parts inside when I picked it up and shook it. Dottie and I would often have deep pangs of regret after shaking packages; I mean they could be fragile!

We apparently recovered quite nicely from our heart-wrenching guilt, because every year we still did the same thing.

Sure enough, upon opening the special gift, my sister turned in an award-winning performance. She could be a movie star, while she feigned her surprise at the contents of her gift. After opening the package, she wanted immediately to dash off to curl her hair, but that would be a direct violation of one of the old man's endless Christmas rules and regulations. Rules that Moses would be proud of, and rules that would give the old Hebrew laws a run for their money in both quantity and complexity.

"Nah, nah, nah, ya gotta stay, Dorothy, until your brother opens his special gift and Christmas gift opening is ovah."

Yes, the old man's holiday rule number one thousand, twenty-nine clearly states, "Thou must stayeth until everyoneth opens ye special presents, under penalty of forfeit of thou ownest special gift."

When Dottie howled in protest, the old man invoked his tremendous power as Ruler of Christmas Gift Giving, "I can take all of these gifts back ya know! Save me a bunch of dough too!"

Dottie sat back down with only a mild lingering moan and complaint, as the old man reached back into the magic berth behind the tree and pulled out the same package, which foiled my snooping efforts a few weeks earlier.

"Here ya go, Paulie, your special gift," the old man said as he deposited the gift in my eager hands. I immediately and instinctively shook the package a few times.

"Wait 'till I tell you what happened in the store, when I finally found it and brought it to the cash register. The guy there, well, I will tell ya 'bout it, later."

Mum quickly ran over the top of the old man to stop the potential storytelling and she scolded me, "Be careful! Please do not shake it. It is fragile!"

Oh, oh. . ..

I saw Dottie look at me out of the corner of her eyes, and she rolled her eyes a little as she recalled our efforts at pre-Christmas gift identification.

I felt those same deep pangs of regret. . ..

Regrets or not, it was my last hurrah for this Christmas, so without further delay, I tore eagerly at the wrapping paper and, much to the chagrin of dear Mum; I tossed it around the room in a frantic effort to reveal the contents, and unleash Christmas magic upon the Henson household. Paper, bows, ribbons and that annoying nametag, now all gone and torn away.

There it was!

Finally!

Oh, well, huh? What is it?

As I revealed a colorful box, I studied the words, pictures and description on the box, as the tearing away of the wrapping paper slowly displayed what appeared to be a radio. A colorful radio, and the words "Shortwave Radio Kit" magically appeared.

Even Dottie was curious now, and she put down the

strawberry-colored curling iron and leaned in.

"What is it, Paulie?"

I held the box up to show her and she studied the words and pictures, too.

Dottie read the label aloud as she pondered this somewhat mysterious gift.

"Connect and tune into the world and unlock the mysteries of the airwaves! Build this easy to assemble kit and travel the world from your desktop!"

I held the box in my hands, intrigued; it was something that, for some reason, fascinated me. It was not a gift that I had requested; therefore, it was a bit puzzling for me. I kind of was leaning towards a goalie mask, but this was a gift that, for some reason, struck a solid nerve within me.

I looked first at Mum who was smiling widely, and then to the old man who sipped a cup of coffee, while he looked over the rim of the cup at my new radio kit and me.

Finally, the old man provided an explanation. "Yeah, yeah, yeah. I will help ya build it. I built one when I was a kid and was about your age. Had it for years and years. Your grandfather helped me build it, wind the coils and put up an aerial outside. I could even tune in and listen to the Bug games when they went all the way out to Shercargo, Illynoise."

The old man could never really ever say Chicago, Illinois. He rather made up his own adaptation.

"Maybe ya can pick up hockey games from Canada, ya know, at night in the winter, when the airwaves are clear."

Mum nodded her head and added, "That would be nice to listen to. Wouldn't it be nice, Paulie?

Ah hah. Hold on now. Now, you are talking my language there, Dad and Mum. Hockey games from Canada! Oh, yes indeed, this all sounds very intriguing. Suddenly, the world grew a lot smaller. My face lit up.

"Thanks, Dad. Thanks, Mum."

"Do you like it, Paulie? Your father and I were not too

sure about it."

"I love it!

Hockey games from Canada, maybe even Russia! No, because they would not speak English.

The hockey goalie mask could wait. After all, what were a few more stitches? Anyhow, old Doctor Salami worked a deal, and he gave the old man a discount per stitch on me.

Suddenly, my world filled with dreams of tuning in hockey games from far-away places, listening to the play-by-play voices of the radio announcers who were calling the action, while floating mysteriously upon the clear airwaves in the winter air, and constructing radio kits. It seemed very magical to me.

Christmas during this particular year took a very surprising turn. . ..

Chapter 2

Then it Snowed, and it Snowed

Christmas was on a Thursday the year that I received the radio kit. On Friday, we celebrated my mother's English holiday known as Boxing Day. Mum served her famous roast beef and Yorkshire pudding dish, and we enjoyed the bonus visits from relatives, as well as many other holiday activities. It was a great day, and my sister and I received a few more gifts on Boxing Day to round out what proved to be an epic haul as far as Christmas gifts go.

Immediately following the two big holidays, I would sit on the edge of my bed and study the radio kit box. I was under strict orders from the old man not to open the box without him, since he emphasized that, "It had a million parts and you could lose them. Wait for me and we will spread it all out on the workbench and work on it together."

Since I was generally annoying, and I needed to fulfill my destiny as an annoying kid, I endlessly bugged the old man for a time of when the assembly of the kit would occur. The lure of lying in my bed listening to hockey games from Canada was a little too powerful at this point. The Christmas season meant that the old man was deeply embroiled, along with Gramps, in consuming turkey, ham, stuffing, eggnog, roast beef, Christmas puddings and sucking down gallons upon gallons of Big Boulder beer, while telling stories of when they conquered the world.

This year seemed to include some type of extra celebration on the part of the old man and our family. In leaning an ear to our family dinner conversations, I did recall something about the old man receiving a promotion, a salary increase, and a little bonus money for Christmas from the shop this year. Our dad was about as hard a worker as there was in the entire world, so that did not actually come as any great surprise to me.

This was not the time to expect the old man to be able to focus upon small parts inside of a radio kit.

Focusing on his normal life was a bit of an issue right now. . ..

Back in this day and time, New Jersey was a hotbed of manufacturing. It was a time when we actually made things here in this country. The old man was a machinist in a machine shop, which made parts for military aircraft. The shop where he worked was similar to many other production shops in the area, and they all closed for the entire week of Christmas until New Year's Day.

It was a magical time for me in my memories.

My father looked forward to this time of the year more than he looked forward to any other time. It was his time to relax, sleep past four in the morning for a change, and a time for very little stress in his life. He deserved the time off.

It was a delightful occasion and the feelings that this week gave to me, I can still feel within my heart to this very day. When the old man came home from his last day of work on Christmas Eve, sat his lunch pail down on the cabinet in the kitchen, and proudly announced that he was off work for ten days or thereabouts, you could just feel his joy.

The entire family shared in his joy, too.

Relaxing on this particular Christmas, while singing happy Christmas songs and sampling the eggnog, might be a little difficult, because the Saturday after Christmas . . . it hit.

It started snowing a little on the day after Boxing Day,

around four or so in the afternoon. Out of the sky, they slowly spit, those types of very fine snowflakes, where the flakes are so tiny, that you can just barely see them. Silently and somewhat ominously, they drifted to the ground. I was in the driveway, doodling around with a hockey puck when the snow began. For me, this type of mindless shooting passed the time, and I was gently shooting the puck against the front wall, which lined our front sidewalk and the edges of our driveway, and then fielding the rebounds. I looked up from my practice with the hockey puck when I noticed that the old man had wandered along.

It was bitterly cold, but there was absolutely no wind, the flakes continued to drizzle out of the sky straight and fine.

"Oh boy, this is gonna be a big one. Look how fine it is starting. When the snow starts out this fine, ya are in for trouble. Can you smell the snow in the air, Paulie? Ya can smell snow like this. It smells wet and dry, all at the same time."

I stopped shooting, captured the puck up on the end of my stick blade and gently tossed it in the air towards the old man. My father was not a hockey player, but in his day, he was a remarkable baseball player, and he caught the puck deftly in his right hand, without missing a beat.

He smiled and gently tossed it back to me.

I caught the puck and tucked it in my coat pocket, smiled and stopped to look up at the sky. Sitting back on my heels, I had to agree with my father. There was no doubt that you could smell the snow in the air. My father's brilliance at teaching me things that he knew and learned from a lifetime of experience, is something of which I could never imagine putting a price to, or living my life without. His remarkable insight in practical advice, common sense and knowledge was a gift from God to me.

Even teaching me the fact that you can smell snow was a remarkable gift.

I thank God every day that he gave me the father that he did.

"Within an hour or so it will be intense. I do not have to go to work, but I am gonna need your help in clearing the driveway. You are big and strong now, and there is no reason that you cannot shovel snow for hours upon hours. It will build those muscles for chasing those damn hockey pucks."

"No sweat, Dad. I will help."

"Ya bet ya ass, you will help," he said while he walked away. I laughed and smiled at his orders.

For a house on a city lot stuck in an urban setting, we had a long and wide driveway. My father cut it in with hard labor. He used a pickaxe and shovel to dig it by hand; he was not going to deal with parking on a busy city street, and annoying alternate side of the street parking rules, street sweeping rules, and snow emergency rules once he had finally saved enough dough to buy our family a home. Because we only had shovels, snow removal was a major operation. Snow throwers and blowers were a dream that we could not afford.

In many ways, I was better off with my driveway situation, then my best friend, Harry M. Redmond Junior was, over a few blocks from our house on John Street. Harry's dad, the legendary Mr. Redmond and my old man, came from the same mold, and a little blizzard or two did not stop them from going to work. In fact, nuclear war or an invasion of aliens from the planet Zutron would most likely not stop them from going to work, either.

In one incident that remains in infamy to this very day, when they had to make it to work in a blinding snowstorm, and the snowplows did not plow the roads yet, Harry's dad made Harry shovel a path through John Street. Harry shoveled the snow in front of the family car, through very deep snow, while Mr. Redmond sat in the car, occasionally beeping the horn for Harry to shovel faster, while slowly inching forward with each shovelful that Harry tossed aside. The plows had opened up Belmont Avenue; therefore, they just had to make it to the main drag. Mr. Redmond would hear nothing of missing work for a little foot or two of snow in front of a vehicle.

Nowadays, people take off from work for too many clouds in the sky, or for excessive wind, or for heavy rain.

I watched my father walk into the garden shed at the end of the driveway and I followed him. I knew what he was doing without even seeing it. He kept a candle in the shed, an old, red colored wax candle that my mother did not enjoy the scent of when it burned. The candle now was in exile in our garden shed. Now, the sole purpose in its short life, until it finally expired, would be to wax the snow shovel blades to prevent snow from sticking to the blade, (there were no plastic shovels back then) and for waxing the runners of our sleds for maximum speed while gliding down the slopes.

Sled adventures of my childhood were many, and those stories, I will leave for other pages down the road.

I stood in the doorway of the shed, watching the old man.

"Gotta wax 'em up, otherwise the snow sticks on the blade and it is a real pain in your ass. It is really gonna snow. I bet ya!"

And snow it did.

The old man's prediction was dead on, because about an hour or two later after he noticed and pointed out the fine flakes, the snow picked up in intensity, until it was snowing so hard that you could hardly see your hand if you held it directly in front of your face.

I loved it.

The cold, the snow, the excitement of a Christmas blizzard stirred my very soul.

It still does to this very day.

Henson snow removal operations for my father were as

if he was going into battle. His eyes danced in his head, he dressed in layers, with sweatshirts underneath heavy winter jackets, a wool hat perched upon his head and heavy gloves, in which he mysteriously called, "firemen gloves" were the choice for his hand protection.

I became a duplication of my father and I dressed the same as he did. Now, the fact of the matter was that I did not have the same pair of gloves, but instead, I used old work gloves with a cloth layer underneath them. I did, however, have to admit that even when being outside in the bitter cold and snow for hours and hours, I never became cold.

"Dressin' in layers is the key, Paulie. Yup, it is, when ya gotta stay out for hours in the cold!" The old man bellowed as he taught me.

I loved the cold, and the snow, as well as the energy of working hard alongside my father, in what he deemed to be, "Emergency, blizzard operations."

It was thrilling!

The trick, according to the old man, was to keep going out in the storm, "To knock the snow down every hour or two, so that the snow does not become too deep. Ya got to figure out how to hold up ovah the long haul."

It made sense to me. The snow removal operations went on in endless waves. You dress, you shovel, you go back inside, and you put all your wet and cold clothing next to the boiler in the basement to dry.

Mum would have the trusty kitchen radio, sitting upon the countertop, tuned to the local A.M. radio station, WPAT in Paterson, while the station's weatherman provided weather related reports on the latest progress of the storm. She would provide us with the updated weather news whenever we came inside to eat and to warm up a bit.

"They are still saying two feet of snow, dear," she would sadly announce, as my sister and I lamented that such a huge storm had to hit when we were off school for the Christmas break, anyway!

This snow was even a bit too much for our beloved, on and off, pet cat Pussface, who alternated between being a stray tomcat and returning to his roaming ways, to staying with us permanently. As he grew older, he spent more time on our back porch hanging out and sleeping in his bed in the far corner of the porch. Since Skippy the terrier and Pussface did not exactly get along so well, Pussface called our back porch his home, which was not too bad. It had a small, cast iron radiator, and while it was not as warm as the inside of our home was, it was a lot better than some box in a dark alley. Pussface rode this storm out, content to mooch a few meals from Mum to eat. He would sleep and he would scrape about in his litter box when he had to, and hang out on the back porch to escape the rough weather.

Oh yes, just to reach the supreme qualifier for his hobo status, he also drank a little beer on occasion. Since it was Christmas, Pussface could also celebrate the holiday when the old man poured some beer into his new dish.

The stories of Pussface the cat would fill up many pages. Suffice it to say, he was a hobo cat, who loved the old man for saving his life on a Christmas Eve, with even worse weather than the storm we were currently embroiled in.

As the snow progressed, the city snowplows continually rolled up Belmont Avenue, and the old man shook his fist at the snowplow driver, who was smoking a big cigar and earning triple overtime on top of his union wages. The driver of the snowplow couldn't care less, as he flew by and closed off the mouth of our driveway with piles of deep snow, about four seconds after we had just cleared the snow out from his last pass.

"DAMN BLASTED SNOW PLOWS! IGNORANT SON OF A BITCH!" The old man would stand in the knee-deep snow at the base of the driveway and furiously shake his fist at the snowplow driver.

"Just once, I want that cigar smoking dumb-ass to jump out of that truck. I will kick his ass all the way back to. . .."

The base of the driveway was hard work to clear; the snow was wet, deep, dirty, and heavy. The salt thrown down upon the city streets had some melting properties within the folds, and it was not easy to toss the snow into huge piles alongside the throat of the driveway. The trick was to place the snow piles on the opposite side of the direction in which the plow rolled by. That way, the snowplow would not push the snow quite so badly across the driveway opening. The old man waved in the air with his shovel and lectured me as he taught me the intricate strategies of snowstorm fighting in the city.

I was big and very strong for my age, and as the snow grew deeper, you required superhuman strength to toss the snow on top of the ever-increasing higher piles of snow.

Soon, my father and I were working in and amongst cavernous piles of deep snow. Our home, our driveway, and the family car sat deep within a bowl of echoing white walls. On a break to rest, eat, and warm ourselves, my father made the fateful suggestion.

Perhaps, it was due to the monotony from the endless cycles of snow removal, with a continuous pattern of warming up, eat a little, rest, only to go back out again in a few hours, or maybe, it was his plan all along, but he said, "Say Paulie, why don't you go and get the radio kit. While we are in the house here waiting for the snow to get deepah, we can at least open the box, check the parts, and study it."

Honestly, his proposal caught me a little by surprise, but once I grasped his suggestion, I nodded my head and eagerly dashed off to my bedroom to grab the radio kit. Skippy, our old family terrier, whose main occupation these days was to sleep on my bed, looked up and yawned at me. Skippy watched me pull the radio kit out, jumped off my (our) bed and decided that he would follow me as I went out of the room. I guess even ole Skippy wanted to see what the eagerness and excitement of which I conveyed were all about now. With a wide smile, I met the old man in the living room and he waved us to the basement.

"We will use the workbench downstairs. It has a lot of room and good light. Now, Paulie, listen up! Ya gotta listen to me on this. Might be a bunch of little parts and if we lose one, then we are shit outta luck. So, calm down and relax. We have to take our time so that we do not mess this up."

I nodded my head and down into the basement, we went. With a wide and somewhat stupid smile frozen on my face, I stood on the side of the workbench, holding the box, while the old man laid out a soft cloth on the top of the bench. He explained that the cloth would prevent the cabinet from becoming nicked or marked and the parts would not be so prone to rolling away from us, as they would be if we laid them on the hard surface. It made a lot of sense, and these were some of the little tricks that my father taught me that were priceless.

"Okay, let's open it. . .."

I eagerly slipped my pocket knife under the edge of the plastic and cut off the plastic coating on the box. We placed the box on the cloth and slowly lifted the cover. The lack of a cover unveiled a wonderment of parts, a grey cabinet with a hole for the tuning dial, and other control knobs, as well as bins and bins of parts all wrapped tightly in plastic wraps.

I prayed that my shaking of the box both before Christmas, and on Christmas morning, had not caused damage to the contents. One look and I knew I was off the hook! It all seemed intact and safely tucked under the plastic cover.

"Careful now. First, find the instructions, and then put the cover right back on the box. We need to study the instructions first."

I grabbed the booklet, and while still under the careful

guidance of my father, I closed the lid to the box, and pushed it aside. He pulled up a stool to the bench, and I leaned in over his shoulder. Opening the booklet, the old man scanned each page.

"See, see, see . . . ya gotta check to make sure all the parts are here first. That is the first thing we will do. Go on upstairs, and ask your mother for a few of those muffin trays that she bakes them rock-hard-ass, corn muffins in. Suckers can crack ya choppers into little bits, but don't tell her that! Those pans will be perfect to sort and hold all the parts."

I returned as quickly as I could since after an explanation of the planned use of her pans, Mum bought into the mission and I handed the old man two muffin pans. I followed orders and skipped the comments about her preparation and recipe for the muffins.

"Good. Sit ya lard ass down here and carefully check all these parts in on the list. The booklet will show you how. There is a checklist to double check each part, check it off with this pencil and place each part in a separate bin in the pans. Take your time, no rush. I need a cup of cawwfee, I will go check on the snow, get my cawwfee and I will be back to check on you in a little bit."

The old man jumped off the stool. He motioned for me to take over the seat and begin the mission in which he just gave to me. Skippy, who had been watching and listening to the entire operation, curled up under the stool and nodded off to sleep at my feet. I eagerly jumped in and set to work. I loved it, and just as the old man told me to do—I took my time.

With the old man's warning deeply lodged in my mind, I carefully opened each plastic bag, carefully checked the part, searched the checklist, and counted them. It was fascinating. Resistors, capacitors, tube sockets, glass vacuum tubes and a multitude of other mysterious electronic parts woven into an intricate complexity of radio magic. Once I had checked the part off on the list, I then placed it in the muffin pan. The larger parts, such as the cabinet, the printed circuit board, the knobs and the dials; I checked and then set them aside.

I was lost in the mission and time, and the old man was gone for a very long time.

I almost jumped off the stool when my father reappeared next to me and he asked, "How ya doin' kid?" Skippy jumped up too. I guess that he was lost in his own dreams.

When I recovered, I answered, "Good. I checked all the parts in. They are all there. Nothin' is missing."

I turned and studied my father's face, and he was scanning my work. He picked up the checklist, and smiled. He seemed very satisfied, and his tone and body language sent a little shiver of pride inside of me. I could tell that I had successfully completed my mission.

"Nice, good work. You did well," the old man gently spoke as he finished scanning the work.

"Do we need to go out and clear the snow, Dad?"

"Nah, nah, nah, I did it awwwready. I wanted you to work on this. Snow is finally lettin' up now. 'Bout two feet out there. It is late. Your mother says for you to come up and wash up for dinner. We can pick back up on this tomorrow. The rest is easy. Building this will not take us long at all. We will start after we clear the snow in the morning."

The old man patted me gently on my back, and then he reached out his hand for me to shake it. I took his hand, and he squeezed my hand hard.

I squeezed it back . . . just as hard.

"Good work today, not only on this, but on helping me in the snow. You are big and strong now. You will be a powerful man. Ya are growin' up, Paulie. Someday, ya will clear snow with your own children and maybe build something for them or with them too."

I only smiled because I was too proud to say anything without tearing up. In retrospect, I never had worked so hard, gained such satisfaction, as I had on this snowy day, while working alongside my dad and earning his pride in me.

The old man waved and pointed to the stairs to go up for dinner. I jumped off the stool, Skippy followed me, and we both went to follow him, when the old man stopped halfway towards the staircase.

He turned and said in a much louder and commanding voice, "Ain't ya forgetting something?"

I stopped and stood there, a little puzzled.

The old man reminded me, "Don't forget to drain the water off the boiler. Add a little water until the sight glass bounces up and down. You know how to do it. I showed ya ass enuff times. It is gonna be bitter cold tonight. We don't need no frozen pipes. If that boiler kicks off in the middle of the night, I am waking your lard ass up to help me get it going again."

"Oh yeah, yeah, yeah. I got it, Dad."

Another mission.

Yes, I was growing up, and it felt pretty good.

In fact, it felt really, really good.

Chapter 3

The Aerial

After enjoying a big breakfast, the old man and I ventured out to clean up the last of the snow. It was now Sunday, and as it so often does, Christmas and the magic of the day started to fade. Pussface the cat, now made an appearance. He was getting porch fever, and he escaped from his warm confines to go on a routine prowl of the neighborhood. He sat on the edge of the top of the driveway, watching us scrape and clear the snow while he cleaned his fur.

The old man warmed up his 1964 Putter Classic Model 200 and knocked all the rest of the snow off the car. We shoveled the snow that fell off the car away and the snow removal mission was nearly completed. The sun was working hard to come out from behind what was left of the clouds, but it was still very cold. Mum warned us to finish early, since the radio station was warning that the day would be clear, but very cold by late in the afternoon. Thankfully, the evil snowplow driver gave up on torturing us. He made enough dough on this storm to last until the next one, and the snowstorm was now a memory too.

All except for the piles.

They reached to the moon, and I had a feeling these piles would be around with us until late March.

Ordinarily, I would be bugging the old man to pull our sleds out and take Dottie and me to the nearby slopes for some good runs down the hill, or now that the snow ended, running over to Harry's house and seeing if we could get an icy and snowy hockey game organized. Not today!

Right now, radio kit fever captured me, and all I wanted to do was finish building the kit. Besides, Dottie locked herself in her room, curling her hair with her new iron and continually washing and drying her hair in new styles. She passed the time by listening all day long to the new rock-and-roll records that she received as gifts for Christmas. We on occasion had to listen to the old man banging his fist on the door of her bedroom, while simultaneously bellowing, "Turn that damn music down! Whoever heard of lyrics about a hard headed woman? What kind of horseshit is that?"

Oh well, good tidings of comfort and joy. . ..

When I spoke to Harry on the telephone, he said he was busy shoveling mountains of snow with his old man too, and afterwards, he was going to build the glow-in-the-dark monster model kits he picked up for Christmas, therefore, any hockey games would need to wait a few more days.

After all the hard work on the snow, we all seemed very happy and content to stay inside, where it was warm and cozy.

We all had our individual missions!

Before I knew it, the old man and I were back at the workbench and beginning the actual assembly of the kit. The mechanical work such as mounting screws, nuts and bolts, the old man watched me carefully, but he let me perform. I was very good with my hands and could handle hand tools well, so that was a snap for me.

When it came to installing the electronic components, my father took the lead. He carefully showed me how to install the various components, to bend the wires and slip them into the holes drilled in the printed circuit board. Then, after he heated up his soldering iron, he taught me how to solder them to the board without creating a mess, or even worse, a dreaded short circuit.

"Make sure that you always use radio solder for this kind of work. This here stuff," the old man said, while holding up a roll of solder. "Ya gotta make sure it is rosin core solder, or what they call radio solder and not the acid core stuff. The acid core is for plumbin' and the radio will not work too swift, if ya blow it and use the wrong stuff. It just will not last too long, cuz the connections are not right."

I nodded my head and made a mental note of the lesson. In the back of my mind, I marveled at the amazing knowledge that the old man had accumulated on such a tremendous variety of subjects. Actually, I made mental notes of that lesson and a few hundred more. We went on working together on the assembly of the radio for hours, and eventually, the old man let me solder a few of the connections. At first, because I was nervous, my hands shook like leaves in the wind, but once I made a connection or two, it became a lot easier.

"I am gonna wind the coils, ya see. It is an extra tricky part. You watch carefully. Your grandfather taught me this part. Hand me that round thing there. They call 'em iron cores and then hand me those red and white wires. Read the instructions there and tell me how many turns on each one of 'em."

I handed my father the requested parts, watched as he carefully held them in his hand, and he made sure the wires were straight and flat.

"Ten turns on that one there, Dad. The other coil is twenty turns."

Years of working as an expert machinist had fine-tuned my father's hands. He could pick up a piece of metal and tell you the exact size of it by feeling it in his fingers. Many times, he would show his remarkable ability to feel the thickness of a part and then use his micrometer to confirm what his fingers already knew. This intricate operation was easy for him. I watched while he worked as skillful as a surgeon does, carefully counting and winding the fine wires around an iron core.

We broke for lunch and when we resumed our work, it became apparent that the kit was nearing completion. The muffin pan bins were now almost empty of parts, the checklist had reached the end, even the "go back and double check your work, in case you blew it" box had a check mark next to it.

The final steps were to plug the vacuum tubes into their sockets, assemble the board inside of the cabinet, string a little dial cord for the tuning dial . . . and . . . finally! The radio was complete.

I felt just a tinge of sadness that we had actually finished the assembly of the radio, but the joy and excitement of testing the radio out ran a ramshackle over those feelings.

The old man read the last step on the checklist aloud, "When you are ready to test your radio, first plug it in, then carefully turn the on and off knob to the "on" position. The dial lights and vacuum tubes should light up and glow, and after a short warm-up, you should hear a rush of noise in the speaker or headphones. If you smell any smoke or see any signs of a malfunction, such as sparks or fire, then unplug your radio immediately."

He looked up at me and screwed his mouth up a little with a frown.

"Damn, that sounds kinda dangerous," the old man said as he looked at me after reading the rather ominous warning from the instructions.

I shrugged my shoulders as the old man regained his confidence and shook his head while somewhat proudly proclaiming, "That ain't happenin' here, Paulie. We got this sucker together right."

"Sure, do hope so, Dad. I would hate for my Christmas present to go up in smoke."

The old man continued to read the final steps from the

booklet, "For proper operation and to hear distant stations in foreign lands, or as radio operators label it, DX, then you will need to install an outside aerial to pick up weak and distant signals. The copper wire and insulators included with this kit should be strung outside, as high in the air as possible, while remaining free and clear of any metal objects, which will cause poor interaction of the radio signals with the aerial."

My father smiled widely. His eyes flickered and his ears twitched a little.

He softly said, "I love putting up aerials. Your grandfather and I put mine up. My old man taught me, just like I am teachin' you, all the tricks ya need when ya are puttin' 'em up."

He then picked up the booklet and without saying a word, he set the booklet down for me to read it too. The old man pointed at the picture depiction of an aerial and he tapped the drawing with his finger.

I peered in and studied it.

The drawing displayed a wire strung between a tree in the yard located in the rear of a house, and the house itself. One end of the wire was in the tree, and the other end, next to a window on the house. The "house" end of the wire entered the window and plugged in the back of the radio. A man and a young boy sat in front of the radio, with wide smiles on their faces, headphones over their ears and together, they were tuning the radio.

In my mind, I knew they had to be tuning in hockey games from Canada.

It just had to be.

It was all so alluring. . ..

In the drawing, on each end of the wire, was a block with two holes drilled on each end, one for the copper wire, and the other for a string to support each end of the aerial. The drawing had arrows pointing to the blocks and called them out to be "insulators."

I assumed that the insulators were the two ceramic blocks, which my father currently held in his hands, along with large rolls of copper wire, which I determined to be the aerial wire. It appeared as if it were fairly simple, except for the fact that there was two feet of snow on the ground out in our yard, we only had one tree which was actually located on a neighboring property, and to top it all off, outside right now, it was about five degrees with a rapidly setting sun.

I knew my father; to him, this was the perfect setting to install an aerial. Nothing stopped him. Not the coldest of days, the most bitter of winds or the blazing heat and sun. When there was a mission at hand, the old man just took the elements to be an additional challenge. As badly as I wanted to tune in hockey games from Canada, I just knew that this Henson adventure was going to be a winner!

He jumped off the work stool and with the aerial parts in his hands; he dashed over to a box on the floor where we kept assorted objects and he frantically dug around in the box. He pulled out a ball of light twine, the kind of which you would tie up packages with, and then he ran over to another box and pulled out a roll of masking tape.

"I need one of your hockey pucks. We can get one out of the box on the back porch."

"No need to do that, Dad. I have one in my pocket right here."

I reached down in my pocket and pulled out the puck while shrugging my shoulders.

"Shoulda figured . . . normal kids don't walk around with hockey pucks in their pockets! Ya got hockey pucks on ya brain, kid."

I took that as a compliment.

While standing here in our basement workshop, I thought about how I should take just a moment to analyze the evolving scenario . . . two feet of snow on the ground, bitter cold, a roll of twine, masking tape, a hockey puck, and my father and me!

Yup, this is going to be a good one.

"Grab ya boots, hat, sweatshirt, and ya heavy coat from in front of the boiler. We are going out, and judging by how many times the boiler has kicked on while we have been working here, it is very cold out there. We have about an hour of light left. C'mon! We can leave the radio there."

I nodded, hustled over and put my snow-fighting garb back on, while my father donned his equipment too. Now dressed for battle, we hustled upstairs and rushed through the living room.

Mum was sitting in her chair, next to the glowing Christmas tree, next to the old man's famous Christmas village (another famous adventure) listening to Christmas music, while she tranquilly sipped on a glass of red wine. She smiled for a mere second, until she saw how we were dressed, the items we were carrying, and a stark realization set in her mind. She knew her hopes of an hour or two of relaxing on a quiet Christmas weekend before we ate our dinner was now lost in a maze of wires, insulators, and dreams of tuning in hockey games from Canada.

"Are you going outside? I was hoping that we could relax a little before dinner."

The old man stopped in front of her chair. He first looked at me, and then how he was dressed, and answered Mum with a somewhat smug reply, "No, we are not going outside. We are coming upstairs to sit with you dressed like this."

Mum put her wine glass down on the end table and she folded her arms across her chest.

Oh, oh. . ..

"I can see that! Let me guess, the radio is finished and you are rushing outside to put up the aerial. Just as you did with your father. It is all you have talked about since you opened that kit. Putting up the aerial. And a little snow, ice and bitter cold, means nothing to you, eh?"

The old man smiled and his eyes darted back and forth in his head like windshield wipers in a cloudburst.

"Ya got it, baby! Nuthin'! Perfect weather for aerial installation! C'mon, Paulie. This will only take a few minutes. It will be easy. Forgive me, honey. We will be in for dinner and maybe layder, honey baby, I will chase ya around the kitchen table too!"

I heard my mother sigh; she knew when the old man uttered the words, "It will be easy" that it was actually the kiss of death on a job.

Years and years, of the old man related adventures, had groomed her for whenever the old man said those fateful words that it was going to be easy that it actually meant for her to prepare for and to count upon disaster.

Out the back door we went, out into the cold. The dryness of the afternoon hit you right away in the lungs. It was the kind of dry cold that sucked all the moisture out of your throat and lungs. I could see puffs of warm breath from my father's mouth as he stopped on our back walkway and studied the tree located just over the fence line, on the now vacant restaurant property next door to our home.

The restaurant closed a year or two earlier because the owner said the neighborhood was so full of crime that no one felt safe any longer and he closed his business. The property now remained there, no longer being maintained and falling into disrepair.

Despite working with my father on jobs and adventures since when I first took my first steps, I could not quite put all the pieces of this puzzle together yet. Twine, hockey pucks and the tape made little sense to me, but I knew I was about to find out.

"Okay, Paulie, here is the plan. We lay the twine out straight and flat, peel it down the walkway there and down towards the driveway. We need enough to reach into the top of that tree, ya see. It has to be loose and free so it floats in the air easily without snags. We tape the twine very gently to the hockey puck so it can break away easily if it gets caught or is in the wrong spot in the tree. Then we toss it up and over the tree, and it floats down to the ground. One of the insulators goes on the end of the twine, the copper wire on the other side of the insulator, and we string the aerial out on the open snow, here. We then pull the end of the wire up in the top of the tree and tie it off on a lower branch. The other end, we attach to the house by your bedroom window and push the wire under the window and into your room."

The old man stood there, beside himself with excitement, and he now demonstrated with his arms and hands some kind of tugging motion. It actually seemed logical when my father explained the plan to me, and surprisingly and rather ominously, I thought that I might have actually followed the plan.

"If the puck gets stuck in the tree or the twine lands wrong, we just tug on it and the puck breaks away from the tape and falls to the ground. We pull the twine back and try it all over again. Simple . . . right?"

Hmmm, I do not think so, however, because of the now overpowering lure of dreams of tuning in hockey games in Canada. I nodded my head to feign that I agreed, and it was indeed . . . simple.

"Make sure the twine is not tangled. Hurry! It is gonna be dark soon."

The old man barked instructions at me while I peeled off the twine from the roll and laid it all out straight and true on the sidewalk and driveway, taking extra care to avoid snow and ice piles. I could not handle the fine twine with my gloves on, so I took them off and within four seconds, my fingers and hands had frozen solidly.

I signaled that I had the twine prepared, and I watched the old man take the end of the twine, break off a piece of masking tape, and he taped the end of the twine on the hockey puck. He positioned his feet as if he was a football quarterback looking downfield, and he cocked his arm while he peered into the upper branches of the tree.

"Now watch. I was the best center fielder in baseball that anyone ever saw. I could throw a runner out tryin' to score from deep center field. I am aimin' for that branch way up there, that there, big one. That is why ya gotta do this in the winter, when there ain't no leaves on the tree to interfere with the throw. Do, ya see?"

I nodded my head, too afraid to state that in this entire, very weird adventure that was the first thing that I had heard of, which actually made some kind of sense. In addition, it was very hard to tell what branch the old man was aiming for because there were quite a few of them up there.

Suddenly, my propensity for interjecting logic into our peculiar and unusual situations entered my mind.

"But that is a hockey puck, Dad. Maybe we should get a baseball out of the box on the porch?"

"Nah, nah, nah! Don't worry 'bout it. I can chuck anything. I got me a cannon for an arm. Just like playing centerfield. The Bugs could use me. Last year they were a bunch'a bums"

"Okay, Dad."

The old man shook his arm a few times, loaded, shook it again, and reloaded the cannon. He slowly wound up and let the hockey puck ride. Up, up, up it went, the twine rolling out behind it, while it soared towards Heaven, and then it stopped dead in the air.

We both watched in horror while the scene unfolded before our eyes. The tape broke off the hockey puck, the end of the twine fell into the snow, and propelled by the old man's cannon, the hockey puck continued onward, lost forever more, into aerial installation oblivion.

The old man turned to me to see where the twine snagged and he yelled, "GEEZ! I TOLD YA THAT YA

GOTTA MAKE SURE THE TWINE IS LOOSE."

We turned, looked where I had peeled the twine out, and quickly found the source of why the twine had stopped so abruptly on its journey skyward.

There was Pussface, the cat, sprawled out on his back, playing joyfully with the ball of twine. The old man sighed. It was hard to become mad at Pussface since he was old, but the old cat was happily reliving his youth. The lure of a ball of twine was too much for him to resist.

Between sighs, the old man said, "Go get a'nudder hockey puck. I will run Pussface off and straighten this mess out. I am sure you will find that puck in the springtime over in the restaurant parking lot."

I quickly went into the back porch and grabbed a few more pucks; in fact, I grabbed about ten of them, because my optimism that I would not lose one or two more pucks was quickly diminishing.

Here we go again while once more partaking in this unusual mission of hurling hockey pucks up into trees. This time, Pussface was now sitting on the sideline as the old man showed him the error of his ways.

We replayed the same scene, the windup and the pitch. Off the hockey puck went, the twine sailing freely behind it! UP! UP! UP! And then, then, then . . . we watched as the puck hit a tree branch and the twine wrapped around it seventy-two thousand times in a hopeless tangle. The plan (which initially sounded grand) of giving a mere tug if the twine became tangled, seemed as if it had a flaw in it.

In fact, it had seventy-two thousand flaws in it.

"STUPID ASS BRANCH! WHO IN THE NAME OF HELL PUT THAT BRANCH RIGHT IN THAT SPOT?" The old man yelled out as he tugged and tugged and then tore at the twine, breaking it off about a foot underneath the tangle. The hockey puck hung from the branch on the end of the twine as if it were the executed culprit of some terrible crime. I quickly prayed that God would forgive the old man for his criticism of his creation of branches in trees.

"Get me a'nudder puck!" In the excitement of the action, my father's New Jersey accent kicked into high gear, and he was butchering the pronunciation of words on an almost continual basis.

Twenty minutes later, there were about ten hockey pucks hanging from twine in the tree upon various branches. I tried to tell myself that they were Christmas ornaments, but that was not convincing at all.

It was growing dark; we were freezing and the lure of tuning in hockey games might have been fading just a bit.

"GO GET ME A DAMN BASEBALL! THESE SONS-OF-A-BITCHIN' HOCKEY PUCKS ARE NOT CUTTING DA MUSTARD!"

I dashed off to obtain a baseball.

Now equipped with a baseball, I could tell that the old man was more in his comfort zone. He always fancied himself as good a pitcher as a certain chap named Jim Beaver was. Jim Beaver was his hero pitcher for his beloved New York Bugs, and while the old man set himself for his next attempt, he even took a stance similar to the stance that Jim Beaver took, whenever he stared into the catcher for the pitch sign. The slight variation was that Jim Beaver did not stand in deep snow on his pitcher's mound.

The old man stopped in the middle of his windup, shook his head and said, "Nah, nah, nah, here is the trouble. Peel the roll of twine out this way. I gotta step in the snow and throw it from ovah here."

The old man pointed to a vague location in the snow, stepped into the almost waist high snow, and took a different angle on the tree. This time it took an angle that pointed directly at our home.

I was about to say something of the sort like, "What if the baseball hits the house?"

However, in the interest of self-preservation, I stayed away from those dangerous waters. Because he was now standing in deep snow, it was considerably harder for my father to wind up and step into the throw. He stripped off his heavy winter coat and tossed it to me. It seemed as if the coat restricted him in some manner and the old man needed to be loose for stepping into this throw. And step into it he did, and off the baseball went.

UP! UP! UP!

The baseball sailed high in the air, the twine happily following it, and we both stood with stupid smiles on our faces, watching it sail high in the air and up and over the entire tree.

Well, the old man had cut loose with a perfect throw, and the good news was that the baseball remained stuck on the twine. It did not break loose; it hurtled magnificently through the air, freely like a missile launch.

The bad news was the landing part.

"CRASH! TINKLE, TINKLE, TINKLE!"

I saw Pussface take off like a rocket ship towards the driveway. He wanted nothing to do with this one. Inside, I could hear Skippy barking his brains out, sounding the alert of a possible home invasion of evil predators.

The loud and horrible sound of a baseball crashing through the glass window of our back porch door was a familiar sound to kids of our ages. Throughout the land, in city neighborhoods everywhere, kids suffered through, ran from, and doled out dearly of carefully saved pennies from endless piggy banks, in order to pay for broken windows due to misplaced baseballs, footballs and hockey pucks.

Harry and I knew that sound so well.

Within four seconds flat of the demise of the back porch window, Mum appeared in the bedroom window facing the backyard. She opened the window, and she stuck her head out in the cold air.

Puffs of her anger emitted into the frosty air.

She yelled, "Easy! Simple, eh! We will be inside in a few minutes for dinner, eh! I swear you are nuts!"

Mum angrily shut the window and her head disappeared back into the house. Suddenly, the window flew open again, and Mum's angry face reappeared.

She yelled, "And you can forget about the chasing me around the kitchen table part of this nonsense too!"

Mum slammed the window shut, and this time she was gone for good.

The old man did not answer her, since he had no actual defense for this adventure. He stood there in the snow, his arms and hands held over his head in a victory sign, staring at the twine as it led up and over the tree in a perfect waveform. The other end of the twine, with the baseball still stuck on it with masking tape, was now on the floor inside of our back porch. But hey, he had accomplished the mission.

The old man smiled and said to me, "What a great chuck, huh? Told ya, all I needed was a baseball. Go and get the insulators and wire. I will tie it on the end of the string, pull it over the tree, and tie off the one end. You grab a snow shovel, dig around in the snow for the ladder on the side of the house and bring it to your bedroom window. We will clean up the glass layder. I think I know of a cardboard box that we can cut and cover the hole up with for tonight so that Pussface won't freeze his old ass off tonight."

In a flash, I found the ladder. No more messing around. I needed to put an end to this adventure before we both froze to death or we broke any additional windows in our home.

I did not think we had that much in the way of extra cardboard boxes.

I set the ladder on the side of the house right by my window and the old man scampered up, screwed a little eye hook into the wood frame, and he pulled up the aerial wire.

Now, in the pending darkness, I could see the glowing

copper wire, majestically swinging in the cold evening wind, while the wire gracefully hung in the air over the snow-covered landscape of our small backyard. It glowed with a little reflection of the city streetlights, and in my mind, I could actually see it capturing mysterious radio signals from out of the air.

We were done!

A few missteps, some extra twine in the tree, and a few lost hockey pucks . . . oh yes, a little window mishap, but in the big picture, it was worth it.

For as long as my family owned 182 Belmont Avenue, a few sections of twine hung from the branches of that tree. Most of the hockey pucks eventually dropped to the ground, when the weather and the elements worked at the tape and they finally gave way, but a number of the pucks hung on for a long time.

When the leaves on the tree disappeared in the autumn of the year, it would reveal all of the unusual display. A multitude of random hockey pucks, suspended by the twine and hanging from various tree limbs. It was a comical reminder of the famous aerial installation adventure.

On occasion, relatives or other visitors would come over to our house; they would sit in our back yard and inevitably, they would spot the unusual display in the tree. Some of our relatives and visitors would not say a word, because they knew us, and knew that we were generally weird. However, other people could not resist the temptation. They would ask the old man why we had so much twine stuck in the tree and had numerous hockey pucks hanging from branches on the ends of twine.

"Pop art," the old man would tell them. "Yeah, yeah, yeah, pop art, you see. It was very popular a few years back. I went to this here museum once, and they had a toilet on display on a wooden crate. Honest, they called it pop art ya see, because. . .."

Chapter 4

Static and Memories

We cleaned up the glass, cut a piece of cardboard for the window on the back porch, thawed out, ate dinner, all while, my father licked his wounds over his errant throw, as Mum went on a good deal with some scolding over his lack of "pitching" skills.

"Jim Porcupine you are not!" She scolded him as my sister and I chuckled under our breath.

"Beaver . . . honey, his name is Jim Beaver."

The excitement now was a bit too much for us to handle and once dinner was finished, the table cleared, dishes washed and put away, the great and final moment was finally at hand. We proudly placed the radio on a small table in front of my bedroom window. A table that my mother used for putting out snacks and drinks, "When company comes over." Mum told me that I could borrow the table until the old man and I installed a little shelf under the window to hold my precious radio.

Would the ominous warnings of smoke and sparks detailed in the radio's assembly manual come to fruition? One could not help but have those words stuck in your mind. . ..

The old man opened the window. He reached for the aerial wire, and he slipped it in the room under the window frame. A touch of snow and ice came in on the heels of the copper wire and the old man stuck an old towel under the window frame to keep the cold out.

He took a little alligator clip, grabbed his screwdriver,

and he screwed the copper aerial wire under a screw on the clip, and clipped it to the location marked "Aerial" on the rear panel of the radio.

All the time, the old man was warning me, "Ya gotta remember when a thunderstorm comes in the summer to unhook this clip and chuck the wire out the window. Just in case lightning comes along and hits in the backyard or close by the wire."

I nodded my head. I did forget about it once and yes, that is another story.

All the family gathered around to watch this major event. Gramps showed up, Dottie stopped curling her hair, and listening to her favorite, soul-eyed singer, crooning sad laments over his "hard-headed woman." Mum arrived with her dishtowel in her hands, and since our family pets seemed to have declared a Christmas week truce, even Pussface received a rare pass to make an appearance inside the home. The old cat sat in the hallway peering in from a distance while Skippy lazily watched from his usual perch on our bed and Fritzie the parakeet kept a suspicious eye on Pussface from safely within his cage.

The old man reached over. I thought for a second that he took a deep breath and crossed himself, but I might have been mistaken. He plugged the radio into a wall socket, looked at me and said, "Go ahead, Paulie. Turn it on."

A quiet hush came over the house. A drum roll would have been appropriate. I hoped and prayed that we would not be blowing "Taps" soon. . ..

I nodded my head, reached for the knob, and in the deep recess of my mind, those terrible warning words of the instruction booklet echoed around and around again in my brain. I slowly turned the control knob; I closed my eyes, and ducked my head a little when I heard the loud, audible "CLICK" of the switch make contact. The dial lights immediately lit up, casting a soft yellow glow upon the metal table. Inside the cabinet, the soft glow of the vacuum tubes told the telltale sign that electrons were now running around inside this contraption, which the old man and I had assembled ourselves.

My father and I both unsteadily leaned in, sniffing the air for burning odors, intensely watching for any sparks or flames, and the rest of the gang watched and held their breath. Suddenly, as the tubes came to life . . . a little crackle came out of the radio's speaker, a little sound, some static and some noise!

I put my hand on the tuning dial, and tweaked the knob a little, and as if it were magic, first a man's voice, and then a loud rendition of the beloved Christmas tune, "Silver Bells" echoed throughout my room.

I smiled so widely that it was a wonder that my face did not crack. My father put his arm around me as the rest of the family cheered in the background! The celebration was on full tilt.

It works! It actually works!

"Ya gotta help me fix that window on Monday, kid."

The old man never was one to let a job go for too long.

Gramps cried out, "The bloody radio actually works."

My father shook my hand, and he hugged me. My dad was not one to show a lot of affection to me, only a handful of times in my entire life can I recall such a moment, but every once in a while, he would. I hugged him too, and it was a moment that I will never forget.

The joy of working with him, learning, the old man taking the time and having the patience to teach me, was something that I knew I would always cherish. In looking back, even breaking the window, as well as shoveling all that snow together, made this a special Christmas week and a fabulous memory.

This was really about so much more than just building a radio together. I never spent such a wonderful time with my father, and the joy of that adventure lives in my heart forevermore.

That night, when the cold, Christmas air was clear, and the radio signals bounced around the entire Earth, I knew it was finally time to find what I searched for both on the airwaves and in my heart.

I plugged the headphones into the front of the radio; I did not want to disturb the rest of the house. I knew that it was a weekend evening and I should be able to find a hockey game broadcast out there in radioland. This was my chance to fulfill my Christmas dream.

Very slowly, I tuned across the radio band, stopping at each signal that I heard. I inched my way slowly across the dial, the glow of the tubes and the dial light guiding my path. Once up the dial . . . nothing, and then back down the other way, then slowly up the dial once again.

I heard something, maybe it was a little crowd cheer or so I thought.

Or was it?

Maybe my brain was guiding my ears. I stopped, tweaked the knob, pressed the headphones to my ears, and I listened carefully.

A wide smile came over my face, as I heard the radio announcer say, "McClure picks the puck up from behind the net, he skates around in his own zone, picks up speed, eludes a defender and passes it up the right wing to Randolph. Randolph is in the clear, he charges down the right wing, he winds and shoots and—he scores! Oh boy, his first professional goal ever! Welcome folks everywhere to the garden rink in Toronto, Ontario, Canada! WHAT A GAME SO FAR!"

Yes, what a game indeed.

Many a cold day, I spent fixing my aerial when the snow and ice came and knocked it out of the air. Then I spent many a winter evening tuning that old radio, listening to hockey games from Canada and stations in other faraway places.

It was, even to this day, the best Christmas gift in which

I ever received, because it was not about just a radio or hockey games from faraway lands but it was about an experience. In essence, it was also about how much I loved my dad and how much he loved me, too.

"What's that, dear Father?" My son, Paul William, asked me, while he looked at an old box that I held in my hands. I had stumbled across the box, while poking around in the attic of the parsonage, as we conducted the annual ritual of bringing down the Christmas decorations out of storage for their once-a-year appearance.

"It is a shortwave radio, Paul William. A radio that I received as a Christmas present when I was just a year or so older than you are right now. I built it with Grandpa Henson. Yup, we built it together, one piece at a time. It was a Christmas week that I will never forget where it snowed and it snowed and it snowed. . .."

I lifted the lid to the box, carefully pulled the radio out, and held it in the air. It looked as handsome and solid as the day we built it. I then reached in the box and pulled the old headphones out, too.

"Cool! Do you think it still works, dear Father? It looks kind of old."

"Sure, it works, Paul William, because we built it to last forever. We used radio solder. The acid solder is for fixin' plumbin' . . . don't ever forget that. If you use the wrong solder, the connections will not last too long. I used to listen in my room at night, with these headphones on my head. Yup, used to listen to hockey games from Canada on it. Hockey Night in Canada on the C.B.C."

The same hockey bug that bit me so long ago had recently bitten our son, and his eyes lit up at the thought of tuning in hockey games from faraway places.

I knew the feeling.

"Wow! Games from Canada, here in New Jersey. Can we try it?"

"Well, I guess, but it needs a special antenna. Actually, I mean, an aerial."

"What's an aerial, Father?"

"A copper wire that you have to put up outside in the backyard, kinda high in the air, in order to pick up the faraway signals. We would need to have an aerial for the radio to work. We can put up an aerial and try it out if you want to."

I looked at my son, and his eyes and smile told the story.

Then Paul William exclaimed, "I sure do!"

"Do you have a baseball, Paul William?"

He seemed somewhat confused.

I also recalled feeling that way once a long time ago.

My son nodded to confirm that he had a baseball, but he asked, "We are going to play baseball, dear Father? I thought we were going to work on the radio aerial."

"No, we are not playing baseball, Paul. Not exactly, Paul William. I will need to show you. It is very, very hard to explain."

I placed the radio back into the box, tucked it all under my arm, and waved for my son to follow me back down the attic stairs. The Christmas decorations would have to wait. Paul William anxiously scampered behind me; dreams of faraway hockey games now invaded his mind.

I also recalled feeling that way once a long time ago.

Once down in the living room of the parsonage, I set the radio aside on an end table, and turned to find Paul William. I clapped my hands together and waved my hands in the air.

"Go and put a sweatshirt on first and then get your winter hat and coat. It is cold outside, and you have to dress in layers if you are going to stay out for very long.

Please tell your mother that we are going to the hardware store. We need to buy a few items to make and install an aerial wire. Hurry because it will be dark very soon. And Paul William, grab my tape measure from the workbench downstairs!"

I watched him nod his head and scamper off on the multiple assignments. He was full of dreams and full of enthusiasm. I knew that feeling, too.

I stood there, and I smiled.

After all, I had better measure the glass window in the back door of the parsonage ahead of time.

Yes, indeed, my father had taught me well.

Thanks, Dad for that, yes indeed, thanks for that, and a whole lot more.

THE END

In the Fields

"I love angels! They are so pretty."

Blue Cloud Redmond, the only child of our best friends, Mr. Harry M. Redmond Junior and his lovely wife, Rose Redmond, admired the ceramic angels in a nativity scene that my wife Binky had set up on a table in our living room. She was about eight years old or thereabouts now, a few years younger than our daughter, Heather Sarah was, and about five years younger than our son, Paul William was.

The Redmonds were always visiting our house, as we often visited the Redmond home too. Indeed, we were all very close. Rose was my wife's best friend growing up and well, Harry and I, we went so far back that at times, it was hard to recall everything that had happened from the day when we first met, when we were both around ten years old.

We had spent a lifetime together. I had only recently begun a project that I had started a long time ago of writing the chronicles of our many adventures together.

I had only scratched the surface.

"Uncle Paul, did the shepherds in the field really, really, really, become that scared when the angels appeared? You said in church on Christmas Eve that the shepherds were afraid. Some ran away because they were so scared."

Blue Cloud boldly stood up, crossed her little arms in front of her chest, planted her feet and firmly stated, "I would not be scared if I saw an angel."

She then turned and pointed at one of the angels in the

nativity scene and happily stated, "Look at how pretty they are. Why were they so afraid?"

Now, I was not actually Blue Cloud's uncle. It was a term of endearment that she used for me. Blue Cloud labeled Binky her "aunt" and likewise, our children used the same terms of endearment for Rose and Harry.

Blue Cloud walked closer to me and asked me a few additional questions that were increasingly more difficult about angels and Heaven and such. Questions that I did not really know the answers to!

She then followed it up with the question that all mothers, fathers, pastors, rabbis, priests, aunts, uncles, teachers, grandparents, and all other adult's fear, when a child of her age asks you. . ..

"Why?"

Oh, oh. The big why question. This could go on for a bit of time.

"Why, would they be so afraid? Jesus being born is a happy thing. Right?"

Blue Cloud might have been only about eight years old and a little bit more, but she was, just as her parents were, smart as a whip! She was wise beyond her years and understood everything. Her vocabulary alone was amazing for a child of her age.

I squirmed a bit in my chair, not sure of exactly why this question came up at all. Suddenly, a multitude of children surrounded me, my own included, as my daughter Heather Sarah and my son, Paul William, zoomed in on me and asked a million questions too. They had jumped on the "Birth of Jesus according to Saint Luke" story too, and they demanded answers.

Lots and lots of them.

I was just not prepared.

It was Boxing Day, the day after Christmas, and it was the biggest day of the year for me. Not only was it a throwback holiday for me to enjoy, ever since I grew up in a household with my English Mum and grandparents who celebrated the day, but now that I was the pastor of a Lutheran congregation, this day was my day to kick back and relax. Especially after working nonstop since the end of October, preparing for the exhausting Advent season.

Advent was so demanding, and there was no escape from it for the church leadership. You would only see certain church families and members on Easter and Christmas, and their expectations were that you would deliver a holiday message and church experience with a dynamic impact, enough impact to last until they decided to show up once again for some type of spiritual renewal.

Mission accomplished this year. It had been a successful year, and our church was growing quite rapidly.

Now it was time to relax!

Every year, we had a big celebration and gathering for Boxing Day over at our house. This year was no exception. The gathering was very casual, informal, and quite laid back. Religion was something that just for one day; I would put on a back burner. I prayed in the morning, I would pray at night, and between those times, well, I would goof off.

The Bible does say everything in moderation.

In addition to our best friends and their daughter, we had a house full of guests. They included my sister and her family, as well as my parents, my in-laws, who were the world famous, Hobnobbers, our facility manager for the church, Mr. Dave Sharp and his wife, my faithful assistant from church, Martha Wiggins and her husband, and a number of other close friends.

I was sitting in my easy chair, in the living room of the parsonage of Reunion Lutheran Church, relaxing in front of the fireplace, which had a good fire blazing along in the hearth, and to be honest, I had dabbled in a bit of sudsy brew during this day too. Now, I was not half in the bag or anything of the sorts, I just was relaxed.

I had read all of Martin Luther's letters to his wife. The letters that he wrote when he was on the road preaching were especially poignant and touching. Especially the letters where he told his wife that the beer that they just paid him with, along with some wages for his work on the road, was not half as good in quality as the beer she brewed at home. Luther's wife was a legendary brewer of German beer and in my mind; she must have been a very special woman.

It was, in my opinion, very romantic.

Therefore, I had no guilt over enjoying a few beers; it was part of my Lutheran heritage. I wonder if Binky ever would consider taking up beer brewing. She certainly was an amazing cook. Hmmm. . ..

It was my day, and I was enjoying it.

We had some Christmas music playing softly in the background. The Christmas tree was all aglow; Binky had prepared my favorite dinner of roast beef and Yorkshire pudding. Binky prepared the dinner with a little assistance from my own mum. All the meal was in accordance with my dear Mum's recipe, along with Binky's fine-tuning. My stomach was full and my head was a little foggy.

Harry M. Redmond Jr. attempted to come to my rescue. "Hey kids, easy on old number twenty-seven. He is not working as Pastor Paul today. Today, he is Uncle Paul and your father. It is his day off now, and I am not sure it is fair to be asking him all those tough questions today. You know, his eyes look a little glazed, his brain clogged up with sudsy delight. Ya know, he is not too focused right now."

Harry gathered his daughter up and held her hand to try to lead her away from the verbal questioning onslaught of me. He was looking out for me as we always did for each other, and while he addressed his daughter, he provided a few words of advice to my own children, too.

We had been friends forever, and perhaps, just a little

more, our connection was very strong and he could sense my moods and body language. I appreciated Harry's efforts, but foggy headed or not, I needed to answer the children's questions.

Besides, now a few of the older folks gathered around me, looking as if they needed to know a bit more about the story, too. Blue Cloud's questions were deep and profound and they admittedly deserved an answer.

"But, Daddy . . . the shepherds," Blue Cloud moaned a bit about the lack of an answer from her, Uncle Paul.

I may be her "pseudo uncle" but I was also a pastor to her, and many others in attendance here tonight. I leaned forward and my wife watched me carefully as she sensed a bit of the pressure that I was under to deliver. I know she felt sorry for me, but she also knew I would always do my job.

Everyone gathered around, and I studied their eyes while I tried hard to find the words to explain.

"Well, gang, you have to understand that when you were a shepherd in the field, it was a tough and dirty life. The shepherds were the outcasts of society, the poorest of the poor, they lived and slept in the fields under the stars within their flocks, and they earned very little money."

I had now attracted attention, even my father-in-law, now turned his attention to me. The abrasive and often difficult Senator William T. Hobnobber, set his Scotch glass aside and leaned in for a listen. I stood by for a general insult from him, yet to my surprise, it never arrived. Senator Hobnobber remained silent. I felt a little clearer in my head now. The cobwebs of the beer-induced fog left me for just a few moments.

"No other people wanted them around. They did not bathe on a regular basis, they had poor appearances, dirty and tattered clothes, and other than their fellow shepherds, they had no friends. It was a lonely life. So, there they were, in the fields, under the stars, just their sheep, some wine, some bread, a meager life. There, they all sat around small fires, sitting in the cold evening air of the desert, under the stars, when suddenly, the sky exploded with heavenly joy. The light alone beaming down from Heaven blinded the shepherds. The heavens opened up, and it was as if the world was ending. Think about it! The glory of Heaven exposed!"

I felt it now, and perhaps the beer was actually helping my passion, because I leaned forward and continued to explain with quite a bit of emotion. Keeping in mind that children, as well as adults, were listening to the message, I needed to make some careful adjustments of the description of the event in order to appeal to everyone.

"You can only imagine how afraid they would be. I am sure a few of them ran off in terror. Some might have had heart attacks and died in fear and shock. Angels suddenly appeared within the explosions in the sky and they told them of the great news. It would have frightened even the bravest of the brave. The greatest soldiers on Earth are no match for the Heavenly Host of the Armies of God. The Bible tells us how one single angel defeated armies of over ten thousand soldiers in a battle. Yet, the shepherds recovered and despite their fear and awe, they did a very simple thing. You see, they believed what they saw was no illusion. It was not the product of drinking too much wine, or a dream. They believed, and sometimes that is the most important thing you can ever do, is just to believe in something or someone you love."

I glanced around the room and now I had a full audience. Not only our children were listening, and studying me, but all the adults too.

"Despite their lowly status in society, they were the first to hear of the birth of Jesus. They believed. How fitting when you come to think about it that the good news came first to the bottom of the barrel, the lowest of the low, and the poorest of the poor. And maybe, just maybe, that was on purpose. Jesus came first to the people who needed him the most. It is just as he told us when he said never to be afraid, for I am with you until the end of all time. Faith is sometimes about never being afraid, but it is also about believing in things that we cannot see, or touch, and would sometimes, be just a little scary."

I finished, and leaned back in my chair.

Harry let go of his daughter's hand and Blue Cloud ran over to me and jumped into my arms.

"I love you, Uncle Paul," she told me as she hugged me around my neck. "If I ever get scared, then I will just think of angels and the shepherds and I will never be scared again! Ever!"

She leaned in and gave me a big kiss. I kissed her too and hugged her tightly. My own children gathered around me now too, and they gave me a hug and kiss too.

Harry came over and patted me on the back.

He told me quietly, "Nice job, there twenty-seven. Even if ya are half in the bag. Ya did well."

"Thanks, thirty-five."

"You know something, Paul? I think sometimes that you are at your best when the pressure is on ya. Sorta like the old days when the pucks were flying at ya, but now, you have a bunch of other kinda stuff flying at you."

He paused, smiled, took a sip of his Wallcrawler cocktail and said, "And ya are pretty good at them both. You were always a little slow on the stick side low if ya were tired, though. That's where I could always score."

He smiled at me again, and in Harry's world of profound but oftentimes a strange logic, I knew exactly what he meant.

I told Blue Cloud as she sat on my lap with her arms around my neck, "I love you too, my dear Blue Cloud, and always remember that because the shepherds believed enough to recover from their fear, we all can do the same. In the fields, watching their flocks by night, and if you think about it, we are all in the fields with them. Now and forevermore, on Christmas Day, as well as every day, we are all in the fields too."

THE END

The Number Fourteen

The number fourteen bus of the city line had a mundane journey. It ran up and down Belmont Avenue, from Paterson to the Borough of Haledon. There was a bus terminal on Belmont, near the border of the Borough of Haledon and the Borough of North Haledon. The terminal served as the main station and it was where the driver took a break, the bus refueled, it turned around and once again; the bus was on its way. At the end of Belmont, the bus turned into West Broadway, made its way over the bridge at the river, and into the downtown section of the city of Paterson, New Jersey, where it stopped in front of city hall, only to turn around and make the trip once again.

Endlessly.

The city bus lines ran endlessly.

They chugged up and down the roads, a little less on weekends, even less on holidays, but it seemed to be that the buses ran endlessly. The buses were a sense of comfort for the residents of the area. They became part of the landscape, part of the atmosphere, and it was reassuring to know that they were always there to bring you where you needed to go. If you did not drive, or your car was broken down, the bus was there, and for a few bits of coins dropped in the old spinning meter, they could bring you to wherever your heart desired.

You could go anywhere; you just had to start on the bus.

These were the days before the big box shopping malls appeared in the suburbs of the cities. The downtown areas of the old city had all that you ever needed or desired. The bus brought you there, and it brought you home too.

The bus drivers all knew your name, and your children's names and your dog's name too. They were as if they were part of the neighborhood, too. The drivers were old friends to share some general conversation with, and to smile with every day. You could always say and wave hello to them as they passed by. Most everyone, even the drivers, ignored the official sign mounted ominously above the driving post warning riders, "Please do not speak with or distract the driver."

In addition, you knew all about the bus driver's families, too. You knew their wife's name, their children's names and the names of their dogs, too. They taped and hung pictures of their lives on the dashboards of the bus, and along the metal visors above their heads, and they proudly mounted pictures of beautiful, smiling women and cute children all over their driver's compartments.

You see, we all need reminders of why it is that we do the things that we do to earn a few coins in this world.

The bus was stifling hot in the summer and freezing cold in the winter. It had a string alarm above the seats that you could reach up and tug on, in order to signal the driver to stop at a location in which you wanted to get off. In many ways, if you ever took a ride upon the fourteen bus, then you never actually left the bus. There was no matter if you rode the bus only once a year, or if you rode it every day, then in your mind, you rode it forever.

Of all the grand days of the three hundred and sixty-five days, Christmas Eve might be the grandest day of them all. People seem to be in brighter spirits, they say hello to strangers, wish one another a happy time, and smile.

Mr. Benjamin Howe was at the steering wheel of the number fourteen bus for this Christmas Eve tour. Mr. Howe was the lead driver now for the number fourteen, having taken over the shift about three years earlier when the dynamic and popular driver, Mr. Roy Kinney, retired after being at the helm of the fourteen for twenty-five years. It is never easy following in the footsteps of a legend, but Mr. Howe filled the role admirably. Benjamin arrived on duty at seven o'clock in the morning, relieving the overnight driver. His bus was ready to go, full of diesel fuel, cleaned and ready to roll. He put his lunch pail under the driver's seat, tucked a picture of his girlfriend in the sun visor above his seat, and he was ready to go.

Benjamin knew this would be a busy day. Last-minute shoppers would climb on the bus to run downtown and pick up gifts they forgot, or just procrastinated on procuring, until the last minute. All of these missions in the quest for the perfect Christmas Day celebration. Benjamin finished his shopping the day after Thanksgiving. He only had to buy one gift this year. After that one purchase, he had no more money left, anyway.

This year was going to be an extra special Christmas celebration because he had bought an engagement ring for the young woman who stood smiling in the picture above him. His hope and prayer, after saving those previously earned dollars and spending them for this ring, was that her answer would be a resounding "Yes" to his marriage proposal. Tomorrow was the big day, and his heart raced a little in anticipation of the moment. It was hard to admit, but he had some doubts as to what her answer might be. After all, he was asking a very lovely young woman to marry him, and he was only a lowly bus driver.

Right for now, he had to run the bus up and down the road, two trips per hour, about sixteen in total, and with a gentle push of the clutch into the floor, and after moving the gearshift, Benjamin started the first trip of the day.

It was cold, but clear weather. At least there were not any ice patches or snowflakes to contend with; there would be traffic, but no ice or snow.

Benjamin rolled out of the terminal. He steered the bus

behind a few cars and made his way through the gears and down Belmont Avenue. The first stop picked up Mr. Williamson, on his way to his job at the headquarters of the bank, and then on the next stop, he picked up Mrs. Twininger on her way into her job, at the large office building on the corner of Broadway and Main Street in the outskirts of downtown. The drivers knew everything about their rider's lives. Some small talk, exchanges of a merry Christmas, talk of their plans for the holiday. It was all very pleasant. Benjamin did not reveal his secret about the ring he planned to give and his big day, just in case of the chance that she decided not to accept.

The number fourteen picked up a few more regulars, all people that Benjamin knew, and people with an extra twinkle in their eyes and a Christmas spring in their steps. Christmas Eve will do that for you.

Benjamin was very used to keeping an eye out on the side of the road for potential bus riders, or runners as the bus drivers called them, as they would wave him down or try to obtain his attention, as well as keeping an eye on the traffic in front of him. It was an acquired skill, and darting his eyes back and forth from the sidewalk side of the street, back to the road, became a second nature to him. He often laughed when he found himself doing the same practice as he drove his own car, as opposed to his bus. His brain had to disconnect and flip-flop from his job to his personal life.

The number fourteen bus rolled away from an official bus stop along the curb, Benjamin pushed the gearshift to the floor, while shifting through three or four gears, and the bus picked up speed. Suddenly, out of the corner of his eye, Benjamin spotted an elderly man waving at him from the sidewalk. The man held a walking cane in his right hand, and he lifted it in the air and signaled to Benjamin that he wanted a ride. Benjamin waved back to acknowledge that he saw him. Parked cars lined the street and since this was not an official bus stop, Benjamin put on his safety flashers and slowly glided the bus to an open spot along the sidewalk. Technically, Benjamin did not have to stop and accommodate the rider's request, since it was not an official bus stop. However, this was an elderly man. It was Christmas Eve, and Benjamin Howe did not care too much for stuffy rules and regulations. Many of the riders on the bus looked up, and no one complained. After all, they all recognized that this was an old man, and he was doing his best not to delay the ride.

The bus rolled to a stop, Benjamin reached for the door lever, opened the door, and he signaled for the man to take his time. Within a minute or two, the elderly man clamored up the steps of the bus, smiled, and dropped a few coins for the fare into the spinning bus meter.

Benjamin did not recognize the elderly man.

He was not a regular rider.

A blast of Christmas chill came in with the elderly man, and Benjamin quickly pulled the doors to the bus closed.

The elderly man thanked Benjamin for waiting.

"Why, thank you, young man. Thank you, so very much for stopping for me, driver. I thought that I had missed you. Merry Christmas Eve to you."

Benjamin nodded and mumbled, "Take it easy now. Be careful. Sit down, there."

The old man nodded. He waved his cane and immediately took the seat directly behind Benjamin.

"I am so sorry to hold everyone else up," the elderly man said as he wiggled on the seat, trying to get comfortable.

"No trouble, old timer . . . it was no big deal at all. Merry Christmas and hold on there," Benjamin said, as he checked the elderly man and his status, checked for oncoming traffic and then pulled the bus away. The elderly man nodded, smiled, and said hello to some of his fellow passengers. He tipped the old hat that he was wearing in the direction of Mrs. Twininger, and she smiled and nodded at his gesture. The elderly man was dressed in a black-colored wool overcoat, with just a hint of mothballs surrounding it; he wore a pressed white shirt, with a red necktie, black trousers and a pair of low top black boots on his feet. His face was not clean-shaven; he had a thin white beard and just a hint of a white mustache lining the top of his smile. His face was so white in appearance that it was hard to see his facial hair. The glow in his eyes reflected his pleasant demeanor, and it was easy to see that this elderly man was friendly and congenial, and above all, he seemed very happy. Perhaps it was the spirit of Christmas in the air, or perhaps it was something else.

He carried a wooden cane, with a bright silver metal tip at the end. If you looked very closely at the crook and turn of the handle of the cane, you could see carved initials inlaid into the wood. They were there, carved a long time ago, so faded that one could easily wander into the supposition that the cane might be a family heirloom, handed down to the elderly man from his grandfather, to his father, and then to him.

"C. E. R" were the letters, now fading and worn, but still visible.

It was just another ride on the number fourteen bus on a Christmas Eve, or was it? Sometimes, in life, the simplest experiences can be the most profound and last a lifetime and even longer.

The number fourteen rolled along, a few more stops, one person climbed off, and three more climbed on, and just before Burhans Avenue, on the corner bus stop near Cook Street and Belmont, a young woman climbed on the number fourteen. She hustled onto the bus, paid her fare, selected a seat opposite the elderly man, looked around and she sat in the seat quickly.

The newest rider on the number fourteen bus was a beautiful young woman, dressed in a winter jacket, a turtleneck sweater, and she wore tight, rather form-fitting, black dungarees. She had long, wavy dark-brown hair that tumbled down past her shoulders, and her hair laid in curls and gentle ends upon her overcoat. In the dancing sunlight of the windows of the moving bus, her hair reflected a hint or two of red highlights here and there. The young woman's appearance was striking, and even dressed in heavy outerwear and clothing to combat the cold and offset the chill, you could detect her slim and trim, yet shapely female figure.

The young woman nodded and smiled at the elderly man. To be honest, she could not help to smile at him because he seemed so kind and gentle. She thought to herself how the elderly man looked very dapper while he sat there in his hat and coat and held his cane tightly in his hand. All the riders held on and swayed in gentle waves in their seats as the bus rocked and rolled while it wove along the city streets.

The elderly man tipped his hat to the young woman, while he smiled back, and then he asked her, "Are you going Christmas shopping? I must say, you are a lovely young lady. Your eyes are sparkling in Christmas excitement and anticipation. Perhaps, it is that you are on a Christmas shopping mission for someone special in your life."

The young woman looked away for a brief second. She was a bit embarrassed that her excitement was so transparent, even to a stranger, but then she felt it was harmless conversation with this kind man. Besides, she could no longer contain her exuberance. She quickly admitted to the man her goal for Christmas Eve.

"Why, yes, I guess it is easy for you to tell that I am very excited. I am shopping for that one perfect gift for my new boyfriend. We have only been dating for a few months, but he is so amazing that I want to pick out something extra special for him."

"Oh, yes in-deedy, how I recall that wonderful thing

known to this world as young love! A new love, my goodness, it is no wonder that you are so radiant."

The elderly man was now caught in the excitement of her quest. He tapped his cane a few times upon the metal floor of the bus, as if to signal his own enthusiasm for her Christmas Eve mission.

While they spoke, Benjamin half-heartedly listened to the conversation, and he looked in the rear-view mirror, when he heard the noise of the cane tapping upon the floor of the bus. Benjamin smiled; he rather enjoyed the elderly man's reaction, too.

The bus stopped while a few riders walked off and some new ones came on board. The bus slowly moved from the end of Belmont Avenue and turned onto West Broadway. The downtown sections of the city of Paterson loomed on the skyline now. You could see the taller buildings, poking above the residential houses lining the road, and along with the skyline, came a long line of holiday traffic, all headed to the same location.

Benjamin leaned over his shoulder and turned his head slightly while keeping an eye on the road.

He spoke to the elderly man and the young woman with a slight smile, "I hope you are not in a big hurry. Holiday traffic already."

"No, young driver. I do not know about the rest of these people, I am sure they are not all retired as I am, but I have all day. I do have some business for tonight, but right for now, I have plenty of time. It is Christmas Eve, of course there is traffic." The elderly man was unfazed by the slowdown of the bus. He turned his attention back to the young woman and asked her, "So, for this special gift. What did you have in mind?"

She answered immediately and without hesitation. "That is the trouble. I do not have a single idea in mind for an extra special gift. You see, my track record with men is not too swift. I am only thirty-six and have already been divorced twice and left a long line of loser men behind me. Now, this new man in my life is so extra special to me. Therefore, I want to make sure I do not ruin our first Christmas together, by picking out a terrible gift."

The young woman, initially, seemed very surprised at her strange and completely honest reaction to his question. She was slightly askew after revealing so many personal details of her life to a stranger on the number fourteen bus. However, there was something very different about the elderly man, which forced her to feel so comfortable and to speak without any inhibitions at all. Perhaps it was his gentle face or the sparkle in his eyes. On the other hand, perhaps, it was something else which invoked her reactions.

The elderly man sat back in his seat and he rubbed the whiskers on his chin. His clear blue eyes wandered around the bus for a time, but he did not speak. The young woman studied him as if she was hoping that he would be able to suggest a special gift.

Benjamin, who had been listening from the driver's seat, and now leaned his weight on the steering wheel of the bus as it crept along in the traffic, piped up, "I know what ya mean. Gift givin' is the same thing over and over again. I usually get the same things. Ya know . . . it is a new tie, a new shirt, some after shave lotion, or a new watch. It is not easy to pick out extra special gifts. I stink at picking out women's clothes. Therefore, I try to go with the perfume route or jewelry and pray that she likes it. It is so hard to pick out something special. I am lucky this year because my gift to my girlfriend is very special. Something that I hope that I never have to give again in my entire life."

Utilizing the extraordinary gift of woman's intuition, the young woman surmised from Benjamin's conversation what the gift might be that he was giving this year and she smiled.

Jumping into the conversation with some enthusiasm,

she said, "Oh my! My goodness, well, good luck with that one!"

The elderly man, too, had followed the hint. He smiled and responded, in what was almost a soft whisper, "She will say, yes."

Benjamin almost spun his head around in surprise that the both of them picked up on his obscure hint, but the traffic forced him to stay focused on the roadway.

The young woman nodded and continued, "I bought my new boyfriend a watch for his birthday last month, and that was a huge success, but it is now crossed off the list. Now, I have no ideas. I just kinda figured I would browse the stores until something special stood out for me."

It seemed as if the conversation would drift into small talk, or fade away, when the elderly man leaned forward on his cane. He spoke in a gentle tone, just loud enough that Benjamin, if he strained his ears, could hear him above the bus and road noises, but it was difficult.

Apparently, a thought had captured the elderly man's feelings, and as he spoke, he conveyed it, "My wife and I were married for sixty-two years. She was lost to this world and me a few years ago, in the late summer, on a golden day, where the sunlight touched every corner of the bedroom. When she passed away, it was as if the angels themselves came down to escort her to Heaven. I miss her every, single day."

He paused, and his eyes momentarily lost their sparkle, but he quickly regained them.

"After we were married for one year and the honeymoon ended, she gave me a glass jar for Christmas. It is a fantastic glass jar, it is curved and tall, and green and red with facets of cut glass that capture the light and reflect colors such as a prism does, all around the room."

The elderly man now sat back in the seat. He spoke louder, and his face broke into a smile, "My wife, she told me that there would be no more Christmas, anniversary, birthday, or other types of gifts. She told me that she did not need anything in the world, except for me. I was all that she needed for a gift. Instead of silly, wasteful gifts, we instead came up with a new way to give each other joy. We vowed to put a coin, be it a penny, or a dime, a quarter or even a dollar bill in the special jar, every time we kissed, we hugged each other; we told each other that we loved each other, or I am not ashamed to say, because I was a lot younger, when we once again demonstrated and honored our love. When the glass jar filled, we would sit and roll the money into paper rolls and deposit the savings in our bank account. Do you know what? We made a down payment on a house with that money that started in the glass jar, we put our child through college with the money from the glass jar and most importantly, we built, demonstrated and honored our love and lives together, with a simple Christmas gift, of a colored glass jar."

Benjamin did not know what to say. He was stunned at the testimony of the elderly man. The young woman reached in her purse, and she took out a tissue as she wiped her eyes of tears.

The elderly man smiled, he laughed a bit and then he said, "Do not cry, my dear, unless they are tears of joy. You have found your soul mate. I can tell by the sparkle in your eyes."

He tapped his cane on the floor to make sure that Benjamin was listening, while Benjamin was driving and the elderly man said loudly, "As have you too, young driver!"

Turning back to the young woman and resting his cane upon his lap, he explained, "I had a soul mate that I was lucky to have for sixty-two years. You know, you can have more than one soul mate in this world. I had many women that I could say that I loved, but I only had one woman that I adored more than life itself. When you find that one special person, gifts mean nothing. They only serve as clutter in our lives. What matters the most is the gift of your love. Love conquers all, and a simple glass jar can represent that better, then all the Christmas gifts in the world can."

The traffic picked up. Benjamin had been so lost in the incredible testimony of the elderly man that his foot jumped on the clutch and the bus jumped ahead as he tried hard to catch up with the traffic. He waved his hand in the air in a signal to apologize to his riders for the sudden lurch ahead of the number fourteen bus. Benjamin was usually such a smooth driver.

The young woman leaned back in her seat and she did not know how to answer the elderly man, except to say, "Thank you. That was the most amazing Christmas story that I think that I have ever heard. Your wife was a lucky woman to have had such a man, and you were lucky to have her for so long. I can only dream of having such a romantic relationship. I think I know now what it is to purchase and to give him as a gift."

The elderly man only smiled. He tipped his hat once again to the young woman and leaned back in his seat.

The young woman leaned forward and asked Benjamin, as the bus crawled over the bridge and into the outskirts of downtown Paterson.

The young woman asked, "Driver, you know this city as well as anyone does. . . is there a store that would sell specialty gifts, such as fancy glass jars?"

Benjamin smiled and leaned back as he shifted gears and answered, "Sure, sure, sure, look in Meyer Brothers, corner of Washington and Main. Two stops up. No need to tug the cord. I will stop."

"Thank you."

No one else spoke, and the bus finally made it through the long line of holiday traffic. Benjamin glided the bus to the corner of Washington Street and Main Street. Many riders jumped up from their seats to leave the bus at this stop, and a long line of riders waited at the corner to change places with them. The young woman waited for most of the riders to pass and exit the bus. She then stood up, went over to the elderly man, leaned over and smiled at him while extending her hand. The old man reached up and gently clasped hers.

The young woman held onto the old man's hands, while asking him, "Are you staying on the number fourteen? Do you have holiday plans for today?"

"Oh yes, I am riding just a little longer. It is so pleasant that I rather wish that I could stay longer on this old bus. I do have some plans for this evening."

"Well then, please accept my wishes for a merry Christmas to you, and thank you for sharing your story, and wonderful ideas. I will never forget you or this bus ride on a Christmas Eve."

"Thank you, my dear. Merry Christmas to you and I hope that young man realizes how lucky he is to have such a lovely woman in his life."

She smiled. He tipped his hat to her, and she moved to the front of the bus and said, "Thank you," to Benjamin as she went to step off the number fourteen.

Suddenly Benjamin had a thought.

He waved his hand in the air towards the young woman and said, "Say, excuse me, but do you plan to take the fourteen-bus back to Haledon, between now, and say, um, four o'clock today?"

"Why, yes. I plan to pick up this special gift and then return to Haledon before it becomes too crazy around here. Why do you ask?"

"If it is not a huge imposition, could you pick me up a glass jar too? I trust you and trust your judgment. Whatever you think is nice. Here is twenty dollars. I hope that is enough. If not, please let me know. If it is less than that in cost, then just keep the change, for your time and trouble."

The young woman smiled and laughed while she took the money and said, "Of course. I will be glad to. Did you ever know a woman who did not enjoy shopping when a man pays for it? I will be sure to catch you on the ride back. I will make a good choice for the both of us and be sure to return to you any change."

She waved and climbed off the bus and a new load of riders climbed on in order to continue deeper into downtown. The bus finally pulled into the end of the line at the huge turnaround in front of the City Hall of Paterson. Many riders walked up the main aisle of the bus and climbed off for the final stop of the number fourteen.

The last rider in line was the elderly man, and he fervently shook Benjamin's hand and cheerfully wished him a merry Christmas.

"Have a wonderful holiday, young driver. I am glad you and the young woman enjoyed my story about the glass jar." The elderly man looked up at the picture of Benjamin's girlfriend above his driver's post. He pointed, and smiled as he said, "Once again, I am quite sure that she will say yes and accept your love and gift tomorrow. Do not worry."

Benjamin was still a little surprised that the elderly man knew of his Christmas plans and he asked him, "I understand how the young lady picked up on it since they are always tuned to such things, but how did you know about me asking my gal to marry me tomorrow?"

"Oh, I know many things, young man. I recalled your statement about the gift and rather easily put the pieces together. In addition, you have a sparkle in your eye, much the same type of sparkle as that lovely young woman has today. When you live as long as I have lived, you learn an awful lot about people and about life."

Benjamin nodded and asked the elderly man as he slowly descended the bus steps, "Will I see you on the flip-flop?"

The elderly man looked back, held his cane on the steps to steady his legs, and shook his head to indicate that was not the case. "No, I have to take the thirty-six bus now. I am heading north."

Benjamin smiled, waved, and he watched for a little while as the elderly man slowly made his way across the walkway, and he stood in line at the bus stop for his connection to the thirty-six line. Benjamin smiled, and he pushed the clutch to the floor, put the fourteen bus in gear, checked traffic and pulled out from the curb.

Ten years later, on a snowy Christmas Eve, the number fourteen bus slowly made its way down Belmont Avenue on its first roll of the day.

At the wheel of the fourteen bus on this special day, was a new driver, Mr. Larry Macalister. "Mac" as his fellow drivers affectionately called him, had recently become the lead driver of the number fourteen bus, when the former day shift driver, Mr. Benjamin Howe received an important job promotion to a higher and prestigious position within the bus company's organization.

Benjamin Howe now worked in dispatch management in the main bus office in downtown Paterson. Everyone loved Mr. Howe; riders, fellow drivers, all types of people. Benjamin was a popular driver and everyone missed his presence at the helm of the number fourteen bus. Yet everyone was very happy to hear of his well-deserved promotion, especially on the heels of the announcement that Mr. and Mrs. Howe were now expecting their first child.

It was difficult to follow in the footsteps of a legend.

Larry was a little anxious. He wanted to get this shift

over with and start his holiday. He had his lunch pail tucked under the seat, a picture of his girlfriend in the sun visor above his driving post, and he was rolling along.

Larry knew this would be a busy day. Last-minute shoppers would climb on the bus to run downtown and pick up gifts they forgot or just procrastinated until the last minute for, all in the quest for the perfect Christmas Day celebration. Larry only had to buy one gift this year. After that one purchase, he had no more money left, anyway.

This Christmas was going to be an extra special celebration because he had bought an engagement ring for the young woman who stood smiling in the picture above him. His hope and wish, after saving those previously earned dollars and spending them for this ring, was that her answer would be a resounding and emphatic, "Yes!"

Tomorrow was the big day, and his heart raced a little in anticipation of the moment. Right for now, he had to run the bus up and down the road, two trips per hour, about sixteen in total.

On the first stop, he picked up a few regulars and then on the next stop, he picked up Mrs. Twininger on her way into her job at the large office building on the corner of Broadway and Main Street.

"Not too many more rides, Mac." Mrs. Twininger announced as she stepped onto the number fourteen. "I am retiring after New Year's Day, ya know."

Larry smiled, nodded, and once more congratulated Mrs. Twininger on her plans. Some small talk, exchanges of a merry Christmas, talk of their plans for the holiday. It was all very pleasant. Larry did not reveal his secret about the ring he planned to give, and his big day, just in case, his girlfriend decided not to accept.

After all, he had some doubts; he did only earn a bus driver's wage. . ..

The number fourteen picked up a few more regulars, all people that Larry knew, and people with an extra twinkle in their eyes and a Christmas spring in their steps. Christmas Eve will do that for you.

The number fourteen rolled away from an official bus stop along the curb. Larry pushed the gearshift, while shifting through three or four gears and the bus picked up speed. Suddenly, out of the corner of his eye, Larry spotted an elderly man waving at him from the sidewalk. The man held a cane in his right hand and he lifted it in the air and signaled to Larry that he desired a ride. Larry waved back to acknowledge that he saw him. Since the street was lined with parked cars and this was not an official bus stop, Larry put on his safety flashers and slowly glided the bus to an open spot along the sidewalk.

The bus rolled to a stop, Larry reached for the door lever, opened the door, signaled for the man to take his time and within a minute or two, the elderly man clamored up the steps of the bus, smiled, and dropped a few coins for the fare into the spinning bus meter.

Larry did not recognize the elderly man.

He was not a regular rider.

A blast of Christmas chill and a few snowflakes came in with the elderly man, and Larry quickly pulled the doors to the bus closed.

The elderly man thanked him for waiting.

"Why, thank you, young driver! I thought that I had missed you. Merry Christmas Eve to you."

The elderly man nodded. He waved his cane, and immediately took the seat directly behind Larry.

"I am so sorry to hold everyone else up," the elderly man said as he wiggled on the seat, trying to get comfortable.

"No sweat. Be careful there, old-timer. Merry Christmas to ya too," Larry said as he checked the elderly man and his status, checked for oncoming traffic and pulled the bus away. The elderly man nodded, smiled, and said hello to some of his fellow passengers.

He tipped the old hat that he was wearing in the direction of Mrs. Twininger, and she smiled and nodded at his gesture.

For a very brief and fleeting moment, Mrs. Twininger thought that she recognized the old man, but she dismissed the thought as vague or a lost memory. Perhaps she had just made a mistake, when she felt that she initially recognized him. As Mrs. Twininger carefully studied the old man sitting there in front of her, she second-guessed the memory. He seemed as if he was vaguely familiar to her. Then again, after some more thoughts, perhaps he was not familiar at all. Mrs. Twininger half-heartedly pondered it for a second or two longer, and then she shook her head, leaned back in her seat, confirmed the error of her memory and went back to staring out the window of the bus.

The elderly man was dressed in a black-colored wool overcoat, with just a hint of mothballs surrounding it; he wore a pressed white shirt, with a red necktie, black trousers and a pair of low top black boots on his feet. His face was not clean-shaven; he had a thin white beard and just a hint of a white mustache lining the top of his smile. His face was so white in appearance that it was hard to see his facial hair. The glow in his eyes reflected his pleasant demeanor, and it was easy to see that this elderly man was friendly and congenial, and above all, he seemed very happy. Perhaps it was the spirit of Christmas in the air, or perhaps it was something else.

He carried a wooden cane, with a bright silver metal tip at the end, and if you looked very closely at the crook and turn of the handle of the cane, you could see carved initials inlaid into the wood. They were there, carved a long time ago, so faded that one could easily wander into the supposition that the cane might be a family heirloom, handed down to the elderly man from his grandfather, to his father, and then to him.

"C. E. R" were the letters, now fading and worn, but still

visible. It was just another ride on the number fourteen bus on a Christmas Eve, or was it? Sometimes, in life, the simplest experiences can be the most profound and last a lifetime and even longer.

When the bus made a stop along the route, the elderly man leaned in and he pointed at the picture of the beautiful, smiling young woman in the picture above Larry's head.

He softly asked, "Is that your gal? She is beautiful."

Larry smiled at the question and the compliment. Larry tried hard to keep his eyes on the road, as well as keep his enthusiasm in check for having such a lovely young woman for a companion, and he hoped, soon, for his wife.

"Sure is, thank you. Yes, she is gorgeous. I am a lucky man."

The elderly man sat back in his seat. He smiled and it seemed as if his eyes were searching the interior of the number fourteen bus for a memory.

After capturing some words from the Christmas Eve air, the elderly man finally spoke, "She sure is. Always, you need to remind her of how special she is too. Never forget. You know, I was lucky enough to be married to a lovely woman for sixty-two years. Yes indeed, my wife and I were married for sixty-two years. She was lost to this world and me a few years ago, in the late summer, on a golden day, where the sunlight touched every corner of the bedroom. When she passed away, it was as if the angels themselves came down to escort her to Heaven. I miss her every, single day."He paused, and his eyes momentarily lost their sparkle, but he quickly regained them.

"If you can listen and drive, and I will humbly ignore the sign that says I should not distract the driver, then please lean in a bit, and let me tell you what she gave me for a Christmas present one year. . .."

THE END

The Return of the Time Bomb in The Cupboard

"So, Paul, how the hell have ya been?" Ronzo Boatmann asked my father, while we all stood in the living room of the magnificent mansion home of our best friends, Harry and Rose Redmond.

"Great, great, great, I could not be any better. In fact, I am feeling wonderful, Ronzo! Retirement is the greatest. After working for fifty-two years, and getting up at four in the morning, it feels good to sleep in until six!"

The old man pointed and waved around to encompass the entire home. He commented while waving, "Boy, this is some dump that old Harry has here, huh?"

Ronzo nodded. He was speaking with my father as both family and friends gathered for a post-Christmas dinner party gathering at the Redmond's home.

It seemed as if everyone had gathered here this year, my in-laws, my parents, all the world-famous Redmond clan, Harry's nieces and nephews, who now had boyfriends, and girlfriends, and in one case, a husband of their own now.

Time had certainly marched along for all of us.

Everyone was here, even including the world-famous Mr. Redmond, visiting New Jersey from Florida, and Harry's sister Patty, and her husband, George "The Big Spike" Pinia, visiting all the way from California.

My boss, the famous Bishop Von Houten attended, and he brought along his lovely wife, and our mutual friends, Rabbi and Mrs. Goldberg, too.

Some were missing from the gang, Father Mark, and Mr. Porter and Mrs. Porter had passed away, and Jeff Porter married and moved to another state. But they were always with us in our hearts.

It had been a very long time since we all gathered as we were on this special day, and I had to admit, it was a joyous and somewhat tearful reunion, and very special to have all the old gang together once again.

I stood next to my father and mother; with my wife Binky hugging me carefully and lovingly around my waist, as we were both watching the various scenes unfold and listening to the conversations carry on throughout the room.

Binky was sipping hot cocoa; she was pregnant with our first child, so her usual Martinis, (shaken not stirred) were on the shelf for a bit.

I swigged at a Big Boulder beer, while I looked around at the marvelous people who were so special to me, and who all were such a wonderful part of my life.

I could not help but to wonder, how many more times, if any, that we would be lucky enough to share in each other's company, either at Christmas time, or any other time, until time and age started to catch up to us all.

My best friend, Harry M. Redmond Junior, and his new bride Rose, had recently built this magnificent home. Harry was very successful now with his quirky inventions, his successful welding and metal business, as well as his restaurant business, and money was no object when it came to Harry M. Redmond Junior.

He earned it, and we all had come a very long way from our humble childhoods in that old city neighborhood of 20 John Street and 182 Belmont Avenue.

Now, to a certain extent, this particular circle of life was new to all of us. Lately, I had felt a bit of angst with our first child on the way. I was working and feeling my way along, in my new position as pastor of Reunion Lutheran Church. My job kept me busy with many new challenges in my life. However, today, I was at ease in such comfortable surroundings, meeting and spending a joyous time with the people in my life that meant the most to me. Harry and Rose were planning their new lives together, and they seemed quite happy. My father had recently retired; my parents had sold our beloved house at 182 Belmont Avenue and bought a house out in the country of New Jersey that was far away from the dust and grit of the old neighborhood.

Or was it?

Perhaps the old neighborhood never really left any one of us. I suspect that was indeed the case and it would be forevermore. All of us knew that in our hearts that we never left there.

Regardless, I sensed their joy as my parents began a new circle in their own lives.

Now that life was all new and fresh, we were all here to reflect upon our joy at sharing such a long ride, a journey together, and I could not think of any people in the entire world, who I would rather spend the time with.

Mr. Redmond was growing very old. I studied him carefully as he held onto chairs and the tables as he moved about the rooms. He was a bit unsteady now, bent over, but his thick chock of white hair was still intact, and his blue eyes still were sparkling.

What Harry and I owed that man, we could never repay, ever, in fact, not even in ten lifetimes.

"Hey, how about another beer there, Paul?" Ronzo asked the old man.

"Sure, sure, sure, Ronzo. A Big Boulder though, cuz, those damn Dingleberries that ya drink are way too sweet!"

When she heard my father's colorful description of what seemed to be the most despised beer in the world, (except for Ronzo because he loved it) my dear Mum turned and shook her finger at my father while scolding him, "Paul William Henson! It is Christmas time. We have a rabbi, a bishop, and your own son, who is a pastor here, as well as little children scurrying about, and you have to let a few nasty words slip here and there! Now, don't you feel ashamed?"

I could hear Rabbi Goldberg laughing in the background and whisper something about how he agreed with my father's description of the dreaded beer, but even in light of the scolding, the old man remained stoic.

"Nah, nah, nah, I don't. Sorry, Ronzo, but it is the worst shit-ass beer ever brewed. Ain't any other way to describe 'em. Rabbis or bishops or anyone else around."

My mother shook her head and gave up; after all, they have been married for over fifty years.

Ronzo was still laughing at the old man's comment when he returned with their beers, handed it to the old man, and they made a Christmas toast in front of a roaring fire. A fire in which Harry had recently rejuvenated inside a majestic, floor-to-ceiling, stone fireplace.

Two old friends sharing old memories and new times during the Christmas season.

Magic. It was pure magic.

After a long sip of the frosty brew, the old man asked Ronzo, "Say there, Ronzo, do you still make that Christmas concoction of hooch? That bootyungass . . . or whatever it is that ya call it? I remember that Christmas when ya turned the entire neighborhood upside down. You remember the year, ya made it too strong and everyone was bombed out of their minds. Most of them lightweight folks, who sucked it down, had their livers gettin' ready to explode. I think they had to call out the New Jersey National Guard to calm everything down. Paulie wrote a short story about it and he called it the time bomb or sumthin' like that!"

Ronzo laughed because the old man had dug up an old memory, a memory of an incident that remains famous to this very day in the old neighborhood.

The legendary, "Time Bomb in The Cupboard" still has a few people suffering from hangovers, even after all of these years.

In fact, the legend of the time bomb in the cupboard lives on forever, not only on John Street in Haledon, New Jersey, and on Christmas Tree Mountain in Sussex County, New Jersey, but it lives in all of our hearts.

It is a reflection; a grand memory of how special life can be.

"Yup, still brew it every year, Paul. Mixing up the new batch for this comin' year in a few days. In fact, I have a little nip or two with me in a flask here leftover from this year's batch. Have ya ever tried my famous Boryeungous? It is a little strong."

I thought to myself how that was such a gross understatement.

"Nah, nah, nah. Nevah tried it. Hear it is a little rough, but it would be nuthin' for me to swallow down my gut. When I was in the United States Army, one Christmas, I got stuck out west there."

The old man turned and asked my mother a question, and as he typically did, he never waited long enough for her to answer.

"What year was that, Joanie?"

Mum put her finger up to her chin as she searched her mind. "Well, dear, I think. . .."

"I think it was the Christmas of fifty-two! Any who, we were stationed in Fort Whatdayaseeit in Arrowzoner. . .."

My father was a typical New Jersey mispronunciation guy, and he just made up his own words when he could not, or would not, take the time or effort to figure out how to pronounce or speak them correctly.

"That is not how you say it, dear. It was Fort. . .."

The old man, once again, trampled over the words of dear Mum. Binky and I almost laughed aloud as Mum waved her hands in the air in frustration at the aborted conversation.

"Yeah, yeah, yeah, whatever! So, anyhow, we had this

Indian guy, ya know, a real Indian guy in our battalion. He lived off base in Arrowzoner, and he wore one of them headdress things, smoked peace pipes and everything. We got us guys some leave for Christmas, and he felt sorry for us, since me and this other guy from Bayonne could not make it back to New Jersey for Christmas. He invited us to his house for a big Christmas celebration and his old man made this powerful Indian hooch stuff. No one could handle it, but I sipped it right down. Did not bother me in the least!"

"Well now, then give the old flask a sip and tip there, Paul, and let me know what ya think."

Ronzo reached in his back pocket and pulled out a silver flask and handed it to the old man.

Binky looked at me and she whispered, "Should your father be sipping that, Paul? Don't you think that you should warn him?"

Binky had never witnessed the intimate dealings with the legendary time bomb in the cupboard, which I had in my lifetime, but she had heard and read the stories.

Almost simultaneously, my mother and I went to warn the old man, with a loud, "Noooooooooo!"

But alas, it was too late.

Almost as if the entire scene were set in slow motion, the old man set his beer aside on an end table. He courageously took the flask from Ronzo; he unscrewed the top, licked his lips and proudly, and somewhat gallantly, he put it to his lips and took a big swig.

Immediately, my father's previously confident face turned into a face of sheer and utter horror! His eyes rolled around in his head, steam blew out of his ears, and his face turned red, while his mouth puckered up in an intense combination of both fear and pain.

BANG!

It was as if a time bomb went off in his head!

He was in serious trouble, and I ran to grab his arm and

help him, when he suddenly turned and spit the entire mouthful of the volatile mixture into the roaring flames of the fireplace. When the mixture hit the flames, a flame about ten feet long, as if it was a flamethrower, shot out of the fireplace, and the fire singed my father's face! In a flash, his eyebrows turned to mere remnants of whiskers, and what little hair that he had left on his head flashed into melted oblivion. The distinct odor of fire-flashed hair filled the air.

I grabbed him as he coughed and gasped. And Ronzo and Mum, as well as others, gathered around him to check on the old man.

"I am okay! I am okay! Man alive, that damn stuff *is* a time bomb! It felt as if a time bomb went off in my head. Wow! Fantastic stuff." The old man panted for air and continued to gasp in huge gulps as he felt his face and checked his body for residual explosive time bomb damage.

"I told ya, Paul. Don't ever say that I didn't warn ya!" Ronzo told the old man, while he gently patted him on the back and he took the flask from my father's hands.

When we all realized that other than missing an eyebrow or two, and a bit more of hair, but mostly losing his pride to the flames, and that the old man was fine, we all began to laugh. We could not help it, and the old man laughed too.

Soon, the entire gang engaged in rollicking laughter, and then it happened . . . a flashback moment of such joy that it made your spine tingle.

Suddenly, the Big Spike, standing alone in the corner of the room, a little toasted, a bit wobbly, broke out in a loud drunken and slurred rendition of, "Silver Bells."

"Ccccityyyyy sssssidewalks . . . blah, blah, blahhhh . . .," George started us off with a big smile and a bit of a drunken slur.

We all smiled, remembered, and all joined in with the

song, even Rabbi and Mrs. Goldberg, and Bishop and Mrs. Von Houten, all of them, after all, we had to.

It was a tradition.

We all sang the infamous song at the top of our lungs, right there in front of the fireplace, Ronzo holding the flask containing the magical concoction in his hands, his arm around my father, while the old man sang and wiped away what was left of his eyebrows from his face.

When the last verse of the song ended, Patty put the finishing touch on the memory.

She smiled and yelled out, "Don't worry, Mr. State Trooper, wherever ya are! Not to worry about all these drunken bums! I am driving!"

I felt the joy of the past fill my heart.

The reflections of that wonderful time so long ago were mirrors to my past, but they were also lenses to my future.

In my joy at the reflection, I grabbed Binky and gave her a long kiss, and then hugged her until I absorbed her.

After my wife and I had hugged and shared the excitement of the special moment, I then turned to Ronzo and hugged him too, while I said to him loudly, "Merry Christmas, Ronzo!"

He squeezed me hard. The big man looked at me with tears in the corners of his eyes, and he smiled widely, and said, "Ain't this life great, Paulie?"

Yes, it is . . . it sure is, Ronzo.

Merry Christmas indeed!

THE END

Epilogue

Every year, Christmas comes and Christmas goes.

A few short weeks after Christmas, the joy becomes a faint memory. The decorations come down; we carefully pack them away, and tuck them in a storage box in a corner of our home, until that time rolls around again in a year or so.

In the epilogue to my own Christmas celebration, I slowly make my way into my living room. I hold in my hands a little cardboard box that I used to store my Christmas tree inside of, and once I pack it inside, and seal off the top of the box, then I tuck it away on a closet shelf.

I only have a small tree these days, a little plastic Christmas tree that sits upon a table. It is neat and compact, and it is somewhat fancy, with some new, whiz-bang L.E.D. lights that I recently purchased and a handful of ornaments on it.

For me, it is perfect.

With about ten minutes of work, the tree is down, the lights and ornaments packed away. All that I have left now is to chase those pesky plastic needles around for a few days. You know, the needles, which fall off the tree. I usually find one or two needles on the floor in August that I missed. . ..

I stored the tree and other boxes away on the shelf in the spare closet. Everything done for another year!

Yes indeed, every year, Christmas comes and Christmas goes.

I walk into the kitchen, steal a beer from the refrigerator, and grab from the cupboard the new beer mug emblazoned with our new publishing logo on the side of it. I bought the mug for myself as a Christmas gift for this year. Carrying my gift, I head back to the living room and ease down into my favorite chair.

I sit for a few moments and I think. I spin the top off the ice-cold beer, pour it into the mug, take a sip and smile.

It was a quiet Christmas, no huge events or mandatory company parties to attend. I listened to some new music, called a friend or two on the telephone, and wished them a happy Christmas, but for the most part, it was quiet, no visitors, no guests to entertain, no large meals to cook and clean up after. A frozen pizza for a Christmas Day meal worked just fine for me. Yes, indeed, no crazy or unrealistic holiday schedules to keep, or people to disappoint, when I did not call or visit them.

However, this year, Christmas was very special.

You see, I did not receive a giant stack of gifts, or tons of letters or cards, or emails from long, lost friends or family. In fact, I only received a few and I could count them all on one hand. No, this year, the superficial things never arrived.

Instead, I received something much better.

No, this Christmas, I spent a great deal of time reflecting upon all the good times in my life, both in the "long ago and far away" past, as well as the recent past. I thought deeply about all the people who I love, the people I care about, and the people that I know care about me too.

I thought about loved ones and friends long since passed on. I thought about how much that I not only missed them, but how much I loved them too. I remembered their faces, their smiles, their voices, and their kindness. In my mind, I remembered how they touched my life, and in my heart, I hoped that I had somehow touched their lives too.

The reflections were unexpected Christmas gifts that I

could never place a price upon; they meant more to me than any packages, gift cards, new frosty beer mugs or whiz-bang L.E.D. lights ever could. The reflections went straight to my heart, and they came from my heart. It all had a profound, calming influence upon me.

To quote the world famous, and forever immortal, Ronzo Boatmann, "Ain't this life great, Paulie?"

Yes, it is . . . it sure is, Ronzo.

Oh, yes indeed, every year, Christmas comes and Christmas goes.

Another sip of beer leads to another smile, because this year, I know that I received the best gift of all.

This year, I received a gift from my heart.

And dear reader, at Christmas time, or at any other time, a gift within your heart, or from your heart, is the only gift that really counts.

ABOUT THE AUTHOR

If you ask Paul John Hausleben, he will tell you that he is not an author, he is just a storyteller. His mission is to continue to write and tell stories to warm your heart, make you laugh, and sometimes make you cry, just a little. Most of all, he deals in memories, and helps you to remember the good times of your own life, and the special people who touched you along the way. Paul was born and raised in Paterson, and then nearby Haledon, New Jersey, and began writing at an early age. He revisited a writing career later in his life, and he now is the author of a number of novels, compilations, short stories and audio and video works. Most of his work, touches upon nostalgic remembrances of simpler times, and tells the stories of heartfelt, humorous, and special human relationships. Other than writing, among many careers both paid and unpaid, he is a former semi-professional hockey goaltender, a music fan and music reviewer, an avid sports fan, photographer and amateur radio operator. He now resides in Somewhere, U.S.A., but his heart always remains along Belmont Avenue in good old Paterson, and Haledon, New Jersey.

Titles by the same author that you also may enjoy:

The Time Bomb in The Cupboard and Other Adventures of Harry and Paul

The Night Always Comes, Another story from the Adventures of Harry and Paul

Reunion, A sequel to the Night Always Comes and Another story from the Adventures of Harry and Paul

The Autumn Collection

The Christmas Tree and Other Christmas Stories. Tales for a Christmas Evening

The Miracle Tree, Another story from the Adventures of Harry and Paul

The Summer Collection

Special Edition: The Time Bomb in The Cupboard and Other Adventures of Harry and Paul

Takes of the Quiet Stranger in the Black Hat

Geyer Street Gardens
Beneath the Mask of a Hockey Goaltender
Another story from the Adventures of Harry and Paul

Where the River Bends and Curls
In addition, to a few others. . ..
Coming soon?

You may write to the author at ctte27@gmail.com

Published by God Bless the Keg Publishing
Somewhere, U.S.A.

You may write to the publisher at
Godblessthekegpublishing@gmail.com

"Life's simple pleasures are so often the best ones!"

www.ingramcontent.com/pod-product-compliance
Lightning Source LLC
LaVergne TN
LVHW010927110826
845149LV00013B/2511

* 9 7 8 0 9 9 0 6 9 7 9 3 0 *